BERECCHE AND THE WAR

LUIGI PIRANDELLO

Introduced and translated by
Julie Dashwood

*t*roubador

Funded by
THE
ARTS
COUNCIL
OF ENGLAND

Published by
Troubador Publishing Ltd
12 Manor Walk, Coventry Road
Market Harborough
Leics LE16 7BP, UK
Tel: (+44) 1858 469898
Fax: (+44) 1858 431649
Email: books@troubador.co.uk

in association with

Hull Italian Texts
Department of Italian
University of Hull
Hull HU6 7RX
Email: a.d.thompson@selc.hull.ac.uk

Series Editor
Professor A. D. Thompson
University of Hull, UK

ISBN 1 899293 027

Typesetting: Troubador Publishing Ltd, Market Harborough, UK
Printed and bound by Selwood Printing Ltd, UK

Edinburgh University Library

Books may be recalled for return earlier than due date;
if so you will be contacted by e-mail or letter.

Due Date	Due Date	Due Date

CONTENTS

HULL ITALIAN TEXTS

ACKNOWLEDGEMENTS

I would like to thank the heirs of the Pirandello estate for permission to publish this translation, the Arts Council for a generous grant towards publication, Jeremy Thompson of the Troubador Publishing for his help, especially with funding, and forebearance, Peter Graves, Senior Lecturer in German at the University of Leicester, for his expert help on aspects of modern Germany (but any errors are mine) and Enzo Lauretta, who has constantly encouraged my work and invited me to speak at the annual Pirandello conferences in Agrigento. Above all I would, as always, like to record my debt to Alan Dashwood, who lives with my work as much as I do.

A NOTE ON THE TEXT

As the basis for this translation, I have used the text of *Berecche e la guerra* in Luigi Pirandello, *Novelle per un anno*, edited by Mario Costanzo, Milan, Mondadori, ser. 'I Meridiani', 1990, Vol. III, i, pp. 571–622 and I have referred to some textual corrections and notes, on which I have drawn freely, in Luigi Pirandello, *Novelle per un anno. Il viaggio. Candelora. Berecche e la guerra. Una giornata*, edited by N. Borsellino and L. Sedita, Milan, Garzanti, 1994, pp. 347–399.

INTRODUCTION

The individual who is not himself a combatant – and so a cog
in the gigantic machine of war – feels bewildered in his orien-
tation, and inhibited in his powers and activities.
(Sigmund Freud, *Thoughts for the Times on War and Death*,
[1915])

It was the time when my son was to leave for the front. [...]
First our fathers, and not us! now, our sons, and not us! I had
to stay at home and see my son leave.
(Luigi Pirandello, *Interviews with Characters*, [1915])

Berecche and the War is a war novella written from behind the lines by
an author who had never done military service or been involved in mil-
tary combat. Pirandello's narrative filter for the onset of war is a protagonist who, like himself, was not born at the time of the war for the
unification of Italy (Italy's Second War of Independence, in 1859–60)
and was too old to fight in the First World War. His, then, is the perspective of the male non-combatant who, in 1914, lives through and lives out
in himself the tensions, conflict and violence of those times, and who
sees the failure of all his ideals and myths in the face of the general
catastrophe. To put it in another way, this is a novella in which the individual becomes the battleground.

Berecche believes in, and has based his life and identity on, nineteenth-century notions of method, order and discipline, and as all these
structures collapse, Pirandello embarks on a radical questioning of
nineteenth-century optimism and positivism. So the belief put forward
by Auguste Comte (1798–1857) in the forward march of the human
spirit finally founders for Pirandello among the carnage of the war. And
so, in particular, does the historical method of Georg Wilhelm
Friedrich Hegel (1770–1831), which claimed to have discovered a general law or direction of cultural growth and to be able to show, through
synthesis, the real forces that control the historical process. History,
according to Hegel, could enable us to distinguish the significant from
the trivial, and so to concentrate on the significant, but in *Berecche and*

1

the War it is the apparently trivial – the lives of the countless millions who die in the war, that assumes importance. And in another way, too, when Berecche and his friends contemplate the possibility that Europe may lose her cultural and economic dominance because of the war, and perhaps become itself a primitive territory to be conquered, there is a challenge to Hegel's claim to have found a scientifically objective method which could be used to draw a line between advanced and backward nations and developed and primitive civilizations, indeed a reversal, a parodic treatment of it. The universe, as Berecche's son-in-law Livo Truppel discovers, does not function like the workings of a clock, and man is not a machine whose behaviour can be understood through observation and analysis, as Hippolyte Taine (1828–93) and Naturalistic doctrine would have it. Rather, the world of 1914 has become mechanized in such a way as to annihilate notions of evolution, objectivity and humanity. In post-Darwinist terms man is reduced to animal level, and is engaged only in a primordial struggle for existence. In *It Isn't Serious* (*Non è una cosa seria*, a short story he published in 1910 and was the source for his play *But It Isn't Serious* [*Ma non è una cosa seria*] of 1918) Pirandello's protagonist Perazzetti studies the animal nature he finds deep down in everyone, however it has been masked by our superstructures and fictions, and which he calls the "original beast" in the "beast's lair" deep inside us.[1] And the 'brute beast', and the struggle for survival are uppermost in *Berecche and the War*. But if, as Don Cosmo Laurentano says in Pirandello's full-length historical novel *The Old and the Young* (*I vecchi e i giovani*, published in two volumes in 1913, but sections of which had already appeared in 1909) human beings fabricate castles on the basis of hypotheses, of a mere cloud, we should also enjoy the greatness of the human intellect, which however despairingly and against all the odds still keeps questioning, and questing for form.[2] The themes of *The Old and the Young* are the failure of the promises, or myths, of the Italian Risorgimento and the disillusionment of the younger generation with the society which emerged in post-unification Italy. In *Berecche and the War*, too, there is war between the generations, but one caught at the moment of crisis itself, in the chaotic events of 1914.

In this introduction I shall discuss the author and his text, then Pirandello's particular humoristic vision as expressed in his treatise *Humorism* of 1908, an optic from which he invites us to read *Berecche and the War*. Next, I shall turn to the evolution of his protagonist, Berecche, and I shall conclude with a discussion of the collapse of form and identity, in particular as exemplified in *Berecche and the War*.

1. THE AUTHOR AND HIS TEXT

Pirandello wrote the different parts of this novella in three stages during the First World War, probably between 1914 and 1917. He published two of them, initially, as separate stories, and the third as part of a different war story. Then, for the definitive edition of his collected short stories, published in 1934 under the general title *Stories for a Year* [*Novelle per un anno*] he divided the material making up the story we now have into eight chapters, and added his own short prefatory 'Note'. In this 'Note' he fictionally situates the whole novella in the months preceding Italy's entry into the war, that is, at a time of great and often furious political debate marked by shifting alliances, radical changes of heart, some very cynical diplomacy and much rhetoric and propaganda. These were the months following the declaration of war between the two groups of allies, Britain, France and Russia (the Triple Entente) on the one hand and Germany and Austria-Hungary (two of the participants in the Triple Alliance) on the other, during which Italy was gradually drawn into the war.

Her position following the assassination of the Austrian Archduke Franz Ferdinand in Sarajevo on 28 June 1914 and the subsequent declaration of war was ambiguous. She had been drawn into the Triple Alliance with Germany and Austria-Hungary by Bismarck in 1882, but the territory she coveted, Trento and Trieste on her north-eastern border, was at the time in the hands of her neighbour and ally Austria. So when war broke out, on the pretext that Austria had declared war without consulting her and claiming that the Triple Alliance applied only to a defensive war (a claim not entirely borne out by the terms of the alliance), she announced her neutrality. Then the Italian Foreign Minister, San Giuliano, and his successor, Sonnino, decided to negotiate with both sides, to see which would make Italy the better offer. There followed a long internal battle in Italy between interventionists and non-interventionists in which the former, who included the writer Gabriele D'Annunzio, the Futurists, led by Filippo Tommaso Marinetti, and the former socialist turned interventionist Benito Mussolini, who wanted to intervene on the side of the Triple Entente, gained the upper hand. After protracted negotiations, Italy declared war on Austria-Hungary in May 1915, and against Germany in August 1916.

The campaigns, contradictions and shifts of the months of the interventionist crisis in Italy are the immediate public context for *Berecche and the War*, and the voices of the opposing factions in the debate are echoed in the novella. But they are filtered through the verbally and at times physically violent arguments and quarrels between Berecche and his friends, and Berecche and his family. So events are seen, as it were, from below, from the perspective of the group of petit-bourgeois friends who meet in the beer-house in Rome and from that of Berecche's family, which belongs to the same social class. In particular, they are seen from the private, subjective perspective of Berecche, Pirandello's Italo-German protagonist.

He, as Pirandello says in his 1934 'Note', reflects the dilemma of so many others at that time who had been educated in the German disciplines of history and philology, and who had made of Germany their spiritual and emotional home. Graziella Corsinovi gives an indication of the intellectual and cultural relations between Italy and Germany at the time, pointing to the influence of German culture on some of Italy's most influential writers during the Romantic period, including Manzoni, Foscolo, Berchet and Mazzini, and to the huge number of translations of German authors into Italian in the second part of the nineteenth century. So great was the admiration for German letters and learning in Italy in the late nineteenth and early twentieth centuries, she says, that there grew up a real myth of German culture.[3] One of the foremost of those admirers of German culture was the great national poet of the generation previous to Pirandello's, Giosuè Carducci, who included his own translations, among others, of poems by Herder, Goethe and Heine in Book VIII of his New Rhymes [Rime nuove] published in 1887. Interestingly, in his seminal book on Pirandello's aesthetics, Claudio Vicentini points out that, although Pirandello hardly mentions Carducci in his work, the position of the two men in the 1890s, especially with regard to the need for Italian writers to look to their own tradition and to avoid servile imitation of foreign writers, was very close.[4] And also among the admirers, although he does not spell this out in 1934, was Pirandello himself. So in many ways the crisis experienced by Berecche and those he represents, the trauma of being forced to face a Germany which was not that of the great writers, philosophers and scholars, but had 'grown up' to become, by 1914, a leading military and industrial country, was also Pirandello's own.

Pirandello's 'Note' indicates an initial degree of detachment from his character. In the very different historical circumstances of 1934, some ten years after he had endorsed the Fascist regime in Italy (an endorsement he was later to qualify but never to repudiate) and the year in which he won the Nobel Prize for Literature, he suggests two main ways of reading his text. The first is in line with theories he had elaborated early in the century. He tells us that, to begin with, he was almost inclined to laugh at his character. But then he was drawn into his situation and his story, to the point where amazement and ridicule turned to compassion. It is a creative process he had described in his 1908 essay Humorism [L'umorismo], as we shall see later.[5] The second should also

4

be mentioned, although I do not intend to treat it at length. Here, where he tells us that Italy's intervention in the war was the work of the most vital part of the nation and was then accepted by the nation en bloc, he seems, in part at least, to address his potential new readers of 1934. Martin Clark defines the myth of interventionism as "the belief that a tiny handful of far-sighted statesmen, spurred on by a few bellicose intellectuals and some noisy streets demonstrations, had swept Italy into war despite all the efforts of parliament and the Establishment to stop them". Italy's intervention instead, he says, was "actually a 'normal' diplomatic decision, taken by conservative-minded men worried about preserving Liberal institutions and public order", but the 'powerful and tenacious' yet 'disastrous' interventionist myth enabled men like D'Annunzio and Mussolini to claim the 'credit' for the war.[6] Why Pirandello chose, in 1934, to revive this myth can only be a matter for speculation. Both his sons fought in the First World War, and he is possibly paying a kind of tribute to them. But his reference to the intervention campaign, however brief, takes on a much more chilling aspect when we remember that by 1934 Mussolini, who had been in power since 1922, had almost certainly decided to invade Ethiopia, a decision which, when it was announced, aroused little enthusiasm in Italy. Or again, perhaps he is reminding his readers of the outcome of war: the destruction and descent into madness which conflict brings. The 'Note' itself is an invitation to multiple readings. For the moment, we should note some of the ways in which *Berecche and the War* is very close to the autobiographical bone, a consideration which could be applied to much of Pirandello's fiction, as his biographers have shown.[7] As Pirandello himself wrote to his daughter in 1922, his work fed on all the torments of his life.[8] Perhaps, as Cervantes said of Don Quixote (a passage Pirandello quotes in *Humorism*), he found in Berecche someone who ressembles him.

Pirandello was born near Agrigento (then called Girgenti), in Sicily, in 1867. In 1882 he and his family moved to the Sicilian capital, Palermo, where Pirandello finished his schooling and first went to University (he subsequently moved on to the Universities of Rome and Bonn). It was possibly in Palermo that he first came into contact with German culture, as at the time there were important trading links between Sicily and Germany which helped to foster an interest in the German language and German writers.[9] He moved to Rome with the consent of his family, perhaps because his father hoped to detach him from what the family regarded as an unsuitable engagement to his cousin, Lina. In Rome, however, he quarrelled with one of his professors, and went to study at the University of Bonn on the advice of his Professor of Philology, Ernesto Monaci, and he stayed there from 1889 until he graduated on 21 March 1891. The title of his doctoral thesis, published in 1891, was *Sounds and Developments of Sounds in the Dialect of Girgenti* [*Laute und Lautentwickelung der Mundart von Girgenti*]. Like Berecche, therefore, Pirandello was educated 'in the German fashion' in the disciplines of philology and history (which, with philosophy and the natural sciences, were required subjects for the Magister-Examen, which he took before proceeding to his doctorate). Indeed, as Michele Cometa points out, German culture and Germany itself have a particular place in Pirandello's life and work[10]. We could point, among many other possible examples, to his translations published in the 1890s of works by Goethe, Lessing and Eckermann; to his 'German Emperor' Henry IV; to Max Reinhardt's famous production of *Six Characters in Search of an Author* [*Sei personaggi in cerca d'autore*] in Berlin in December 1924; to Pirandello's character Dr Hinkfuss, who is a caricature of a German director, in *Tonight We Improvise* [*Questa sera si recita a soggetto*], which had its first production in Königsberg in 1930; and to *As You Desire Me* [*Come tu mi vuoi*], which is set in Berlin and Udine ten years after the First World War, and is one of his most profoundly disturbing plays.

There are other ways, too, in which the Pirandello who distances himself from his character in 1934 is most anxiously present, in a disguised form, in his own narrative. The war years, traumatic for society as men perpetrated "deeds of cruelty, fraud, treachery and barbarity so incompatible with their level of civilization that one would have thought them impossible", as Sigmund Freud wrote in 1915,[11] were particularly difficult in the private sphere for Pirandello and his family. He and Antonietta Portulano, the daughter of his father's business associate, had married in 1894 and settled in Rome. Their three children, Stefano, Lietta and Fausto, were born respectively in 1895, 1897 and 1899. By then, Pirandello had written a few volumes of poetry, some articles and reviews, some one-act plays (the majority of which he never published), two novels and a number of short stories, and he had obtained a post at a training college for women (the *Magistero*) in Rome. He and Antonietta were, however, financially dependent on the monthly cheque he received from his father and on the income from her dowry, which with his father's capital was invested in a sulphur mine in Sicily. In 1903 their personal and financial circumstances changed radically. The sulphur mine was flooded, and an essential part of their income was lost. Antonietta received the bad news in a letter from Sicily, and when Pirandello returned home that evening he found her semi-paralysed. So Pirandello was faced with the gravity of Antonietta's mental illness and with a serious financial crisis. He had to supplement his meagre salary from the *Magistero* by giving German and Italian lessons, and to find ways of making his writing pay. He also

6

had to continue to teach at the *Magistero*, work he found deeply uncongenial, until 1922, that is, until he began to gain an international reputation as a playwright.

Antonietta slowly recovered from the paralysis, but she began increasingly to show signs of paranoia. She became obsessively jealous of Pirandello's students at the *Magistero*, and during the war years her jealousy and persecution mania became so serious that she thought her daughter, Lietta, was trying to poison her. Even, apparently, she thought that the relationship between Pirandello and Lietta had become incestuous. When Lietta attempted suicide because of her mother's accusations, Pirandello was forced to send his daughter to live with an aunt in Florence. Finally, when his son Stefano returned from the war the family agreed that Antonietta should be institutionalised, and at the beginning of 1919 she was committed to a private asylum in Rome. She remained in this asylum, the Villa Giuseppina, until her death in 1959 (that is, some 23 years after Pirandello's death in 1936). The *topos* of the hysterical woman recurs in Pirandello's fiction, and has been linked to his experience of Antonietta's illness. It is a *topos* which is clearly present in *Berecche and the War*, in the scenes in which Berecche's wife and daughter turn on him, weeping, screaming and threatening, as the author of all their ills. I would argue that, in this novella, as the male protagonist collapses under the weight of his own construction, he too becomes hysterical, then ultimately passive, and that one of the themes Pirandello explores in this story of overemplotted masculinity is the fear of feminization.

Another important theme in the novella is the destruction, almost the dismemberment of the family, which finds its equivalent in the public sphere with Berecche's prescient fears that as a result of the war Germany will be dismembered and torn to pieces. We have already seen how Antonietta's illness threatened her family, and in particular her daughter. Other threats came from what Pirandello's elder son, Stefano, indicates as a collective decision taken before Italy's entry into the war that "we, in the form of my person, should prepare ourselves for the war".[12] Stefano went to fight in the Italian army as a volunteer, and Pirandello's younger son, Fausto, was called up as soon as he was of age. Stefano was taken prisoner by the Austrians in 1915, and he remained their prisoner until the end of the war. Both sons contracted tuberculosis. When Stefano returned, the family agreed to Pirandello's decision to have Antonietta institutionalized, but to do so they had to resort to deception. Giudice says that for years Antonietta had wanted a legal separation from her husband, and she was now told that her wish would be granted, but that before she could achieve it she had to be declared sane. That could only happen, she was told, if she agreed to be examined in a psychiatric hospital, and so she gave her consent to be moved to the Villa Giuseppina.[13]

Finally, shortly after Stefano had left for the war, Pirandello's beloved mother died in Sicily. Her story is told when she becomes a character speaking to an author who is also her son in another of Pirandello's war stories, the *Interviews with Characters* [*Colloquii coi personaggi*], published in 1915. It is a story frequently mentioned by critics, yet Pirandello left it out of the definitive edition of the *Stories for a Year*, possibly because it is so personal in tone. In it, the 'shade' or 'ghost' of the author's mother comes to remind him of the family's Garibaldian tradition, their involvement in the struggle for Italy's independence during the nineteenth century, their exile to Malta and their return to Sicily. She then tells her son that his suffering is perhaps what she feels, as a woman, at not being able to do, but seeing others do, what they would have liked to do themselves. And so, she says, he wanted this war, but if it would have cost him nothing to sacrifice his own life in it, his suffering at the risk to his son's life is immense.[14] Giovanni Macchia has argued that the family nucleus is the dark seed from which Pirandello's multifarious situations spring; indeed, he says, what happens at the political and social level seems to be a projection on a larger scale of what happens within the family.[15] This is clearly apparent in Pirandello's war fiction, as elsewhere in his writings.

2. THE VISION OF THE HUMORIST

In his long essay *Humorism*, Pirandello returns again and again to what he calls the "feeling of the opposite" [the *sentimento del contrario*]. It was a concept he had begun to elaborate much earlier, for example in an essay of 1893, *Art and Consciousness of Today* [*Arte e coscienza d'oggi*], where he gives his views on the place modern science and modern philosophy have assigned to the human race in the post-Copernican universe. Now that the earth can no longer be seen as the navel of a boundless creation, he says, human beings have a melancholy place within nature, and a humoristic poet could well find in this a theme for his poetry.[16] These were ideas he returned to frequently, including, and especially, when in 1905 he wrote an introduction to the first instalment of a novel by Alberto Cantoni. He subsequently republished this introduction with the title *A Fantastical Critic* [*Un critico fantastico*], and he incorporated much of it into *Humorism*. In a much-quoted passage from this latter essay he illustrates what for him is the essence of the art of the humorist by describing the hypothetical case he sees of an old lady whose dyed hair is completely smeared with

8

some kind of horrible pomade, and who is clumsily made-up and dressed in unsuitably youthful clothes. This image, says Pirandello, intially makes him laugh, as he perceives that the old lady is the opposite of what an old, respectable lady should be. And if he wanted to remain on a superficial level of interpretation, he would go no further than this first, comic reaction, as the comic consists in the awareness of the contrary. But the true humorist does not stop here. He reflects on what he sees, and thinks that perhaps the old lady takes no pleasure in decking herself out like a parrot (his image), that indeed she perhaps suffers from appearing like this, and only gets herself up as she does because she is pitifully deceiving herself into thinking that she can hide her wrinkles and grey hair and so keep the love of her much younger husband. If reflection works in him like this, he says, he can no longer laugh, as he has gone beyond, or rather deeper into, that initial perception of the contrary, to reach a feeling of the contrary. The two concepts, of the *awareness of the contrary* and the *feeling of the contrary*, both italicised in Pirandello's text, have become terms of art of Pirandellian criticism, to describe the movement between the comic and the humoristic, the crossing Pirandello wants us to make in the face of incongruities and contradictions from superficial ridicule to understanding and compassion.

This shift in perspective, leading to an awareness of a different reality, also reveals the ambiguities of seeing, the contradictions inherent in our perceptions of others. Crucial to this process is what Pirandello calls the special activity of reflection, which comes to disturb and interrupt any organization of ideas and images into a harmonious form. So humoristic works, and Pirandello cites Sterne's *Tristram Shandy* as a supreme example, are disorganized, disconnected and interrupted by continual digressions. Moreover, he says, this way of writing results from the special activity reflection has in the work of the humoristic writer, leading to disturbance and disruption, association through contraries, and the linking of images not through similarity or juxtaposition but through conflict. Each image evokes and attracts a contrary image, and leads the writer to find new, hitherto unthought-of associations between these images. Discontinuity and the 'doubling' of images are, then, the work of reflection, which Pirandello metaphorizes as a little demon which takes apart the mechanism of every image, every phantasm set up by feeling. And reflection and fantasy work closely together, to the point of seeming almost inseparable. The faculties we usually associate with critical reflection, that is, analysis and judgment, seem to be superseded. Pirandello's 'fantastical critic', as his paradoxical title indicates, makes use of both reflection and fantasy, and together these faculties inform the vision of the humorist.

9

It is interesting that Pirandello's image of the old lady has itself been subjected to 'decomposition', or deconstruction. In an article of 1968, Giacomo Debenedetti wrote that in his example Pirandello violates the most common features of real life, in which wives are usually younger than their husbands. More recently, Maggie Günsberg has seen the whole passage as working covertly to reinforce a cultural stereotype: that of the "distasteful sexuality, or even anti-sexuality, of the post-menopausal woman"; while Ann Hallamore Caesar says that the old lady's dilemma "is the product of a set of highly coded, and very tenuous, social assumptions", of which there is no hint in the example as Pirandello writes it.[17] Pirandello's old lady is certainly grotesque, almost a caricature, in her pathetic and unsuccessful attempt to hide her age, and Pirandello obviously makes her repellent as well as laughable. She is, furthermore, the only non-literary example Pirandello gives in this section of his essay, and the only female 'character'. The others, in turn, are Marmeladov, from Dostoyevsky's *Crime and Punishment*, whose words of drunken protest to Raskolnikov ("My dear sir, my dear sir, [...] my dear sir, perhaps all this sounds very funny to you, as indeed it does to other people, and perhaps I'm only worrying you with the silliness of all these miserable details of my family life, but believe me, it isn't funny so far as I'm concerned. For I can feel it all.") are quoted. So in Pirandello's text, too, he is allowed the dignity of self-justification and feeling. The next is a nineteenth-century poet, Giuseppe Giusti, part of whose poem is also quoted, and the final one is Cervantes' Don Quixote, a character for whom Pirandello feels particular sympathy, as is evident here as elsewhere in his essay. Perhaps his old lady arouses so many contrasting feelings because she exemplifies the many different reactions which Pirandello's humorist can experience: indulgence, sympathy and even pity, but as a feeling of the opposite arising from indignation, spite and mockery, which are just as sincerely felt as the former. In another way, and like the man whose condition Pirandello describes in his essay as bitterly comic, a violin and a double bass at the same time, she is as 'fuori di chiave', as out of tune, as jarring, today as she was in 1908.

As we have already seen, Pirandello's writings abound in image and metaphor, as well as argument, story and example; they are, indeed, whether prose, theatre or poetry, fictional or theoretical, grounded in metaphor, and this takes us to a fundamental aspect of his thought. He was acutely aware of living at a time of great intellectual crisis, as Daniela Bini puts it to be "giving the final blow to an idea of [...] philosophy as order, as systematic thought, responding to the eternal human quest for stability, certainty, and meaning."[18] As he wrote in *Art and Consciousness of Today*, with the collapse of all the old norms, and since new norms had not yet emerged or become established, the concept of the relativity of everything had become so widespread that a fixed, unshakeable viewpoint was no longer possible. Now, he says, that philosophy has shown us that there is no God, and that the Earth is nothing but a minuscule atom, a common or garden little spinning top thrown out by the sun and whirling along the same path around the sun, we can no longer have a precise knowledge or notion of life; only a feeling, which is by definition changeable and varying.[19] He returns to the idea that we cannot know life, but only have a feeling for it, in *Humorism*. The problem, as he elaborates it there in another much-quoted passage, is that while everything in life is relative, and in a perpetual state of flux, our way of trying to make some sense of that flux is by attempting to halt it, and fix it in stable and determined forms. These forms are the concepts, the ideals to which we would like to hold, all the fictions we create for ourselves, and the conditions, the state in which we tend to become established. So 'form' here is equivalent to the construction of our inner and outer life, and is needed intellectually, psychologically and socially, to bring meaning and order to life and to establish an identity, for ourselves and for others. But all of this, as is amply demonstrated in Pirandello's recurring use of terms like (self-) deception, illusion, mask, construction and so on, is just a fiction which allows us to attain some stability, some constancy. Within ourselves, the flux which is life continues, behind the barriers and beyond the limits we have imposed, and at times of crisis the flux of life becomes a flood which sweeps aside the forms we have created to contain it.

These are ideas which, with different shifts and emphases, are thematic in Pirandello's writings. In the universe as he sees it we can have no objective knowledge of our world, ourselves, or others. All we have is our own subjective, sincere but illusory set of constructions, which can be swept aside at any moment. We live, not in reality, or with anything but the slightest possibility of understanding the true nature of life, but by fiction, by metaphor. We are, indeed, the metaphor of ourselves. It is this metaphor which Pirandello's humorist reads, seeing 'beyond' or 'into' it, and deconstructs.

3. THE EVOLUTION OF BERECCHE

The 'case' Pirandello witnessed in 1914 is that of a character who, (apparently) on the basis of one particular scene from his distant past and (certainly) through his own long and arduous studies, has developed theories about how the world should be arranged. He has, therefore, been able to construct his inner and outer self so as to appear, in his own eyes at least, coherent and seamless. The 'method' he has evolved, described in chapter III of the novella, is structured on a dogged and painstaking search for facts, on a belief in the evidence of the senses rather than ideas, on the assumption, for this small, latter-day Hegel, that the pattern or law of history and nature can be understood if there is a proper arrangement of subject-matter (as in Berecche's voluminous card-indexes). As with Thomas Gradgrind, in Dickens' novel *Hard Times* (of 1854), Berecche wants to be a man of realities, facts and calculations. But, as the government officer tells Sissy Jupe in the same novel, to be governed and regulated by fact means discarding the word 'Fancy' altogether, and such a rejection is unthinkable in Pirandello's world. His 'fantastical critic' is only one in the long line of similar embodiments, which include his famous personification of Fantasy (or Imagination), his "sprightly young helpmate" who brings home to him "the world's unhappiest people" to turn into stories, novels and plays in his 1925 'Preface' to *Six Characters in Search of an Author*.[20] Nor is Berecche himself devoid of imagination, as is seen by his love of his garden, his 'poetry of solitude', his ability to see the Earth from afar, and his feelings of protest and rebellion when he thinks that in the War countless millions of troops will be slaughtered, leaving no trace in recorded history. He is, however, caught between his own construction of Germany as his ideal native- and father-land, on which he has based his identity as a patriarch, and the 'inner voice' which tells him that his devotion to discipline has led him to suppress his natural feelings as a father and as an Italian.

Berecche is proud that his surname is based on a corrupt pronunciation of a German name, and indeed it is, but on the German verb 'berechnen', which means 'to calculate' (and not 'to reason', as has sometimes been said in this context). The more tenuous his control over events becomes, the more frequent is Berecche's use of the verb 'to reason'. I would argue, therefore, that although Berecche adopts the 'Philosophy of the Distant' ['Filosofia del lontano'], in common with others of Pirandello's philosophical characters, he exemplifies philosophies which have lost their relevance. A consideration of some of his Pirandellian predecessors suggests that he has lost contact with reality, and reason, to the point of madness.

At night Berecche escapes from his problems into contemplation of the heavens, distancing himself in time and space from the present and from the Earth. In a poem first published in 1887 Pirandello apostrophizes the stars, and asks if there is living on one of them some animal who sees the Earth from afar and likes it.[21] The theme gradually becomes associated with a poetics of seeing via an upside-down vision, illustrated in *Humorism* by the image of looking through the different ends of a telescope. The discovery of the telescope, an infernal machine, for Pirandello, on a par with Logic, was the final blow to our anthropocentric view of the universe, as when we look through the smaller lens, we see as big what nature wanted us to see as small; but while our eye is looking through the small lens, our soul leaps up to look from above through the bigger lens. Thus the telescope becomes a terrible instrument, and the Earth and mankind, and all our glories and greatness, fall away. Humoristic reflection next provokes the feeling of the opposite, and suggests that if we can understand and conceive of our infinite smallness, we are perhaps not as small as we appear through the end of an inverted telescope, as it means we also understand and conceive of the infinite greatness of the universe. However, and the train of never-ending humoristic reflection continues, if we feel ourselves to be great, and if a humorist finds out, we may end up like Gulliver, a giant in Lilliput and a toy in the hands of the giants of Brobdingnag.

Some of Pirandello's protagonists use this constant reversal of perspective to escape into a contemplatory mood, which allows characters to distance themselves from the present by regarding present events as though they belonged to the distant past. Pirandello's poet imagines a stellar animal so removed in space from the Earth that it could find it beautiful. For three journalistic essays written in 1909 Pirandello invented an interlocutor, the philosopher and historian Dr Paulo Post, a name he had already used as a pseudonym when signing two articles he published in 1896.[22] Dr Paulo Post, who is writing a book called *The Philosophy of the Distant*, is the immediate predecessor of Dr Fileno, a character in Pirandello's meta-fictional novella, *The Tragedy of a Character* [*La tragedia di un personaggio*], published in 1911. Both characters, the journalistic and the fictional, think that history is an ideal composition whose elements are assembled according to the nature, likes and dislikes, aspirations and opinions of historians. Because of this, it can never capture reality, where the elements are still de-composed and scattered. In order to find an austere and serene peace, these philosophers look at the present through the larger lens of the telescope, so that the present, as it were, shrinks into the distance. In the case of Dr Post and Dr Fileno, it is a distancing process which allows both of them them to bear the very recent death of a daughter, to free themselves from sorrow and suffering and to take a noble, dignified attitude to tragedy.

Berecche's situation, I would argue, is a reversal of the 'Philosophy of the Distant'. Rather than being a philosopher, and as again is implied by his surname, he is a character trying with increasing desperation, and against all the odds, to convince (or to find conviction). So he organizes his life within two 'frames'. The first of these is the homosocial beer-house, which is itself a copy, however detailed and convincing, just a small piece of the owner's native-land, where Berecche can defend Germany, attack France and Italian neutrality, drink beer, and ostentatiously prefer German wooden matches to Italian wax matches. The second is his flat in via Nomentana, which is also a simulacrum, between city and countryside but in reality neither, and which reads like a synthesis of 'Northern' concepts of Italy (including fountains, pine-trees, cypresses, neo-classical villas, moonlight). Berecche, who imposes a 'German' identity even on his family, including in the names he gives to his children (Teutonia, Margherita; significantly the name of his son, Fausto, is both Italian and contains a possible reference to Goethe) has Romantic longings for the foreign and the faraway. But the difference between Pirandello's novella and, say, Eichendorff's *Life of a Good-for-Nothing* [*Aus dem Leben eines Taugenichts*], of 1826, is that Pirandello is to this extent writing an anti-*Bildungsroman*. Eichendorff's Good-for-Nothing, who sets out for Italy in search of freedom, for release from his dominating and philistine father, then experiences doubts and changes of fortune. Eventually, though, after seeing in Rome the gulf between dream and reality, he marries a good Christian girl and decides to return to that city on his honeymoon. So he finds his identity through the love of an ideal woman. Berecche's situation is the reverse of this. He is himself the dominating, patriarchal father whose authority is undermined, and whose identity, under all the strains imposed on it, collapses. Without ever fully realising it, he is, indeed, a toy in the hands of the giants of Brobdingnag.

So he is led to curse the 'giant' Germany, to witness the final collapse of the promises of the scientific and historical method, and to damn the light of reason, that Promethean spark which Pirandello, in *Humorism*, says illuminates only the vain forms of human reason. He is unable to adopt some of the 'old' solutions, such as finding peace through the light of faith, or (if we accept the position as, again, a reversal) beauty in the view from the stars. The escape into history, however illusory, which is the solution adopted by Don Cosmo Laurentano in *The Old and the Young*, is blocked because Berecche is continually recalled to the present. And the 'pleasure of history', exploited by Henry IV in Pirandello's play of the same name to enable him to continue to live out his fictional life as an eleventh-century German emperor, is denied him. With the final revelation of the failure of systematic thought, and sustaining myth, Berecche is inescapably caught up in the contingent, the chaotic and the catastrophic, and his 'ontological insecurity', to borrow R.D. Laing's phrase, becomes such that he can no longer feel. So, in chapter VII of the novella, entitled 'Berecche Reasons', when Fausto and Gino

14

Viesi have gone missing and with destructive fury his wife and daughter turn on him and all that he represents, Berecche can no longer feel. All he has is an abstract idea of his grief, and he weeps, but like an actor on the stage, just at the idea of his grief, not because he feels it. Some of Pirandello's characters, including Fausto Bandini, the first-person narrator of the novella, *When I Was Mad* [*Quand'ero matto*], of 1902, experience 'divine visions', moments of ecstasy, akin to what Pirandello in *Humorism* calls 'exceptional moments'. They feel, pantheistically, as Bandini describes in detail, that they can penetrate the life of all that is around them, and that they are almost becoming the world, that the trees are their limbs, the earth is their body, the rivers their veins, the air their soul.[23] A precursor of Vitangelo Moscarda, the first-person narrator of *One, No-one and a Hundred Thousand* [*Uno, nessuno e centomila*], a novel finally published in instalments in 1925–1926, but on which Pirandello had been working for fifteen years, Bandini arguably exemplifies one form of the schizoid condition, which Laing found much later in the century in his patient who was threatened with complete absorption into Nature. Berecche's 'moments', though, seem anti-epiphanic. He cannot become one with the trees he walks past on his way home, and objects are, as it were, fetishized. So he feels a "strange, melancholic longing" for the vacated chairs and table he sees in the beer-house, as though they had the malefic power to turn him, with his connivance, into an 'absence', an object. He appears to represent a different schizophrenic condition, in which the paranoiac feels "persecuted by reality itself", and so develops a "false inner self" which "feels it is outside all experience and activity. It becomes a vacuum".[24] Persecuted by reality, yet longing for participation in the world (again like Laing's paranoid schizophrenic), Berecche embarks on a course of hallucinatory self-destruction, which culminates in his (temporary) blindness.

4. THE COLLAPSE OF FORM AND IDENTITY

Pirandello's universe, post-Copernican and post-Darwinian, is one of discontinuity and fragmentation. Pessimism about the place of human beings in a universe without significance or causality permeates his writing, including his essay *Art and Consciousness of Today* (1893), his short story *Little Pellets* [*Pallottoline*] (1902) and his novel *The Late Mattia Pascal* [*Il fu Mattia Pascal*] (1904), as well as *Humorism*. Berecche shares the idea of the world as a "tiny grain of sand", a small planet whirling on through space with no apparent purpose, where the millions of human histories ("stories of mere worms", in *The Late*

15

Mattia Pascal) can simply be wiped out. It is a universe which, for Pirandello, the prevailing literary modes, and especially realism, could no longer convey. In another essay of 1908, *Subjectivism and Objectivism in Narrative Art* [*Soggettivismo e oggettivismo nell'arte narrativa*], Pirandello wrote that art should not be based on a formula, a system, a pretence nor, above all, on a pre-established method.[25] He is here writing against all the contemporary 'isms', and so reiterating his criticism of the different literary 'schools' of his times (realism, verismo, naturalism, determinism, symbolism, mysticism, decadentism) already voiced early on, including in 1893 in *Art and Consciousness of Today*. So in his novel *The Outcast* [*L'Esclusa*], the first version of which dates back to 1893, he parodied the veristic style of the Sicilian writer Luigi Capuana, who was his friend and mentor when he first settled in Rome and the man who persuaded him to turn from poetry to narrative. As Felicity Firth has shown, *The Outcast* was based on Capuana's *Disgust* [*Ribrezzo*], of 1885, but while Capuana's plot is "rooted in causality and characterisation", in the world of *The Outcast* "character is multiple and motivation fortuitous", and dislocation and the principles of distortion and parody are applied to key aspects of the veristic mode.[26] In a reply to his critics which became a postface to the 1921 edition of *The Late Mattia Pascal*, Pirandello defended himself against charges of lack of verisimilitude, and of writing about the abnormal, the paradoxical and the absurd, by saying that life, with all its glaring absurdities, has "the inestimable privilege of being able to do without that very stupid verisimilitude, which art thinks it has the duty to obey".[27] We should now turn to the ways in which Pirandello's mode of telling captures the abnormalities, paradoxes and absurdities of which his critics had accused him.

Berecche and the War is, both literally and metaphorically, a whole series of variations on the themes of seeing and blindness, as exemplified by the first movement of the novella, from the 'outer' street scene (which is Expressionist in its violence and jagged contrasts) to the 'inner', minutely detailed creation by the German beer-house owner. And, with the contrast in styles, colours, shapes, sounds and smells, there is a movement from the 'new' Germany to the old, pathos-ridden, nostalgic image of a Germany which Berecche has made his own. Yet, since the beer-house is in Rome, it is paradoxically both familiar and exotic, and so for Berecche, as from the other side of the counter its owner, the beer-house is *spoken action* [*azione parlata*], their own conscious and unconscious subjective reality. *Spoken action* was a concept Pirandello applied to theatre, in a brief essay of 1899 of the same name, but it can easily be extended to his narrative works as well, as Romano Luperini has said.[28] In his essay, Pirandello writes that "characters should detach themselves, alive and independent, from the written pages of a play" and that "this artistic miracle can only occur if the playwright finds words that are spoken action, living words that move, immediate expressions inseparable from action, unique phrases that cannot be changed to any other, and belong to a definite character".[29] However, the beer-house is also, in my view, another example of the process of 'doubling'. As though from different sides of the looking-glass, from their different perspectives, it 'belongs' to both Berecche and its owner.

Berecche is caught up in his own mental creation, as his friends in the beer-house perceive when they draw a caricature of him as an honest (but humble) pawn, goose-stepping across a chess-board and wearing a German helmet in a game which is marked out by clear rules, set moves and hierarchies. But, as Pirandello said in *Humorism*, the author of a parody or a caricature exaggerates and deforms, indeed creates monsters, in order to laugh at or ridicule blemishes or defects, and may be intentionally cruel. Berecche perceives of himself as a serious, educated person with a well-defined and superior place in society (aggressively superior towards his friend Fongi, for example, as well as towards his family), and he cannot recognise himself in the simplified act of aggression which the caricature represents. Fortunately, and through a characteristic Pirandellian process of doubling (then of tripling), he thinks that the attack is made on Germany, which he can defend, and not on himself, and so he avoids what Ernst Kris calls being killed by ridicule.[30] But the hostile nature of the caricature, the deformation of the likeness which is intended to capture the essence of the subject, is reaffirmed at many points in the novella, including in chapter III where Berecche and Germany become indistinguishable.

What has led Berecche to construct and control his life as he does is the all-powerful memory of watching his father and some friends, forty-four years previously when he was a boy of nine, discussing the Franco-Prussian war as they lean over a map on which they trace the course of that war. It is a memory which disrupts the flow of the text, a typical analepsis in which we see how the nine-year-old Berecche was given access to the 'theatre of war', and allowed to participate in a game in which he joined in the discussions and actions of the adult world. But the game deforms reality. The war is played out on the basis of scant, and out-of-date, information, remote from the scene of action and in an entirely subjective way, as each participant insists on plotting his own route with his finger, so constructing his own war. And, in a complex use of the figure of synecdoche, through the eyes of the child each of the fingers takes on a strange personality of its own. In the game, the horrors of war are, as it were, scaled down to the size of a few, aggressive fingers, and transformed into a source of both entertainment and personal rivalry. However, the fingers themselves become detached from their owners, decontextualised and so 'monstrous' and disturbing. In relation to Berecche's 'mental map' they acquire a power and a fascination which stays with him until his phallic finger eventually becomes powerless to impose authority on his family and so legitimate his status.

David Lodge tells us that the realistic tradition "depends upon certain assumptions, especially the assumption that there is a common phenomenal world that may be reliably described by the methods of empirical history".[31] Pirandello's 'map scene', though, is yet another demonstration (running throughout Berecche as previously in *The Old and the Young*) of one of his central tenets: that history itself is a construction. Like a map, it is dependent on the perceptions, motives, choices and omissions of its makers and interpreters, and the validity of those perceptions is fragile and fleeting. The adults in the scene in the definitive version of the novella appear to have superimposed their admiration for the French Marshall MacMahon, presumably aroused by his victory on the Italian side at the battle of Magenta (1859), onto a very different war, in which MacMahon was forced (in 1870) to surrender his French army to the Prussians at Sedan. In earlier, more explicit versions of this scene Berecche's father is said to be on the side of the Prussians, and the young Berecche to have supported the most aggressive of the fingers. The excision of both pieces of information from the final version makes it much more ambiguous. His father is now just one of the adults who admire the Franco-Italian hero, MacMahon, not the Prussian forces, so if Berecche's responses to this early scene have led him to construct an authoritarian, patriarchal and heroic 'German' identity modelled on that of his father, he has unconsciously made only part of the game his own, and so planned the course of his life in an irrational, lopsided and highly selective way. One of the significant details in his memory of the 'map' scene is of a much-loved object, a clock in the shape of a windmill with one broken sail. This *mise en abîme* is a reference, as had been said, to Don Quixote, who loses his wits from reading too much and filling his mind with impossible nonsense.[32] Like his famous fictional predecessor, Berecche wants to tilt at the 'giant' Germany alongside his son, and like him too he witnesses the collapse of his illusions and ideals.

The irrationality of Berecche's course of action is made plain when he tries to superimpose his memory of that early game onto the First World War, and is forced to see the futility of the new game within which he attempts to plot and contain the very differently horrific, complex and multifarious realities of 1914. As I have said, for Pirandello life always breaks out from the boundaries and limits we try to place on it, and this, in one way, in what happens to Berecche when the inadequacies of his 'method' are revealed, and he feels that he, a retired history teacher of 53, has no hope of palingenesis, no place in the new order of things. Yet his wish to participate is evident in his daydream, early on in the novella, of going to war with his son and Gino Viesi, his future son-in-law, both of whom he calls his 'sons' on either side of him (and with himself in the central position). However his authority, and his authorities, are under threat as life is, as it were, 'congealing' into forms which are at the same time new and, distressingly and ironically, grafted on to the old heroism of the Risorgimento. In his Oedipal struggle with his sons he, the father, is robbed of his legitimacy and status while his sons go off to volunteer, to become war heroes.

The form their heroism takes is at once familiar (they want to refute those who accuse them of cowardice; to show themselves 'worthy'; to demonstrate their patriotism; to find comradeship and come to maturity) and, if we look at the terms in which Fausto writes to Fongi, asking him to intercede with his father, a critique of the interventionist ideology which underpins their actions. Fausto's letter, as Giudice says, contains images and expressions, phrases and concepts which Gabriele D'Annunzio had used in speeches on Garibaldi and the Thousand during the interventionist campaign. For example, in a speech in Rome on 12 May 1915, D'Annunzio had said: "we are not, we do not want to be a museum, an hotel, a holiday resort, a horizon repainted Prussian blue for international honeymoons, a delightful market for buying and selling, cheating and barter."[33] The result, for Giudice, is that the letter "seems like a series of clumsy variations on two or three Dannunzian tropes in a bizarre rhetorical exercise."[34] Pirandello detested D'Annunzio, so his choice of Dannunzian language here might seem another example of critical parody, an ironic commentary on the new calls to heroism. But Pirandello was aware of the influence D'Annunzio's speeches were having on young people in Italy at the time, and he is also showing how Garibaldian myths of his parents' generation, and of his own youth, are being transformed into new myths which sweep away the old order. There is a play on the disparity between rhetoric and fact, on notions of continuity and radical discontinuity. The effect of D'Annunzio's rhetoric, in a conflict which Berecche (like his author, who in an interview of 1915 said that the war was one of machines and economic interests)[35] knows is a capitalist war, fought for economic advancement and not for the sake of great ideals, is ideologically blinding. In what becomes in the text a sombrely ambiguous play on words, Fausto wants to fight in order to show that in Italy there is a "bit of wasted youth", by which he presumably means not simply young people indulging themselves in riotous living (the Italian phrase, as the English, has this meaning) but rather that there are young people whose potential is not being called upon or realised. The tragic meaning in the context of the First World War refers, of course, to the millions of young men who died, and whose youth was literally 'wasted'.

Even though he denies that this is a 'great' war, Berecche cannot contemplate the thought of his son's death, and so he makes one final, absurd and pathetic attempt to join him at the front. In what is a final dismantling of order, method, authority and authorities he secretively (and so with feelings of shame and to avoid ridicule), without telling anyone, studies a manual on horse-riding, and the next day goes to a riding school to ask for a crash course. He uses what remains of his authority to bully the instructor into acquiescence, falls off his horse, remounts, insists on using a whip and, with eyes closed, fantasizes about charging into battle. And in his fantasy he is no longer in the central position but behind Fausto who, wearing a Garibaldian red shirt, outstrips him. He falls again, this time seriously injuring himself, and is taken home with his head and half his face (and so his eyes) bandaged to join the darkness of his blind daughter, Ghetina. Berecche's fantasies have, in a Freudian sense, become over-luxuriant, over-powerful, and so the conditions are laid for an onset of neurosis or psychosis.[36]

In this novella Pirandello uses the semantics of suffering and madness to convey the state of mind of his protagonist and the world he inhabits. The composition of the novella seems almost fortuitous, and its structure is humoristic, interrupted by digressions, analepsis, radical shifts in perspective and multiple viewpoints. Parody, distortion and caricature are used to unmask illusion, including the illusion that the universe can be seen through the lens of systematic philosophy or contained in the veristic mode and its language of cause and effect. Above all, I would argue, it is a chiastic text, and Paul de Man tells us that the figure of chiasmus "can only come into being as the result of a void, of a lack that allows for the rotating motion of the polarities."[37] This void is apparent in the moment when we are told that Berecche's Germany had, until yesterday, been his prestige, his authority in his house; that Germany had been everything for him, until yesterday, and in all his negative experiences – his life lived with no moment of real joy, his suffocating studies, his reduction to rage, fear, guilt, impotence, hysteria and blindness – which are all the polar opposites of what he wanted to achieve. Through his ponderous and painstaking studies, described to us cumulatively through the repetitive and weighty use of the conjunction 'and', he wanted to build for himself a character of coherence and consequence. But the corresponding use of polysyndeton, in the scene where he searches desperately for information about his missing son, shows the oppposite movement: a descent into senility and madness. The final tableau of the novella is of Berecche, temporarily blind, holding his blind daughter on his knee. We never learn what caused Ghetina to go blind, but no matter who wins the war, her condition will not alter. Throughout the novella she has been a waif leaning against a wall, or taken by the hand to prayer, the embodiment of blind faith and passivity. Now that reason has shown itself equally blind, Berecche joins her in a configuration which is in itself a reversal: no longer the grieving mother with her son, but a father grieving with his daughter. He becomes, indeed, a *pater doloroso*, an icon not for life but for death.

NOTES

1. Now in L. Pirandello, *Novelle per un anno*, III, i, ed. M. Costanzo, Milan, Mondadori, Ser. 'I Meridiani', 1990, pp. 123–131.
2. Now in L. Pirandello, *Tutti i romanzi*, II, ed. G. Macchia, M. Costanzo, Milan, Mondadori, ser. 'I Meridiani', 1986, p. 52.
3. G. Corsinovi, *La persistenza e la metamorfosi. Pirandello e Goethe*. Caltanissetta-Rome, Sciascia, 1997, pp. 20–21.
4. C. Vicentini, *L'Estetica di Pirandello*, Milan, Mursia, 1985 (2nd revised ed.), pp. 84–85.
5. The text of *L'umorismo* can be found in L. Pirandello, *Saggi, Poesie, Scritti varii* [henceforth *SPSV*] ed. M. Lo Vecchio-Musti, Milan, Mondadori, 1960, pp. 15–160. The essay has been translated into English as *On Humor* by A. Illiano and D.P. Testa, Chapel Hill, University of North Carolina Press, ser. University of North Carolina Studies in Comparative Literature, 58, 1974. I have drawn freely on both essay and translation in this introduction.
6. M. Clark, *Modern Italy. 1871–1982*, London and New York, Longman, 1984, p. 185.
7. For biographies of Pirandello, see: F.V. Nardelli, *Pirandello. L'uomo segreto*, Milan, Mondadori, 1932; G. Giudice, *Luigi Pirandello*, Turin, UTET, 1963 [there is a translation, which is an abridged version, of this work into English as: *Pirandello: A Biography*, Oxford, Oxford University Press, 1975]; E. Lauretta, *Luigi Pirandello. Storia di un personaggio "fuori di chiave"*, Milan, Mursia, 1980. For biographical surveys in English, see: *Luigi Pirandello in the Theatre. A Documentary Record*, eds S. Bassnett and J. Lorch, Switzerland etc., Harwood Academic Publishers, 1993, esp. pp. 1–17 and my 'Introduction' to *Luigi Pirandello: The Theatre of Paradox*, ed. and introd. J. Dashwood, Lewiston, Queenston, Lampeter, The Edwin Mellen Press, 1996, pp. 1–22.
8. See: M.L. Aguirre D'Amico, *Vivere con Pirandello*, Milan, Mondadori, 1989, p. 13.
9. See G. Santangelo, 'Influenze della poesia dell'Ottocento' in *Pirandello poeta*, Florence, Vallecchi, 1981 pp. 35–36; G. Corsinovi, cit., p. 23.

10. M. Cometa, *Il teatro di Pirandello in Germania*, Palermo, Edizioni Novecento, 1986, p. 359 (there is a translation into English in this volume of Cometa's introductory essay in Italian at pp. 357–372).

11. Now in S. Freud, *Civilization, Society and Religion*, The Penguin Freud Library, vol. 12, London, Penguin, 1991, pp. 57–89 (p. 67).

12. G. Giudice, *Luigi Pirandello*, cit., p. 262, n. 1.

13. G. Giudice, *Luigi Pirandello*, cit., p. 300.

14. This is my translation/paraphrase of the text. The story is published in the *Appendix* to *L. Pirandello, Novelle per un anno*, III, ii, ed. M. Costanzo, Milan, Mondadori, ser. 'I Meridiani', 1990, pp. 1138–1153.

15. G. Macchia, *Pirandello o la stanza della tortura*, Milan, Mondadori, 1981 (2nd ed. 1982), pp. 67–68.

16. *SPSV*, cit., p. 895. See also É. P. Ó Ceallacháin, 'Contradictions and the Doubling of Ideas: Pirandello's Writing on Theatre and the Essay *L'Umorismo*', in *Luigi Pirandello: The Theatre of Paradox*, cit., p. 40.

17. See, in turn: G. Debenedetti, 'L'umorismo di Luigi Pirandello', in *Nuovi argomenti*, April–June 1968, p. 180; M. Günsberg, *Patriarchal Representations. Gender and Discourse in Pirandello's Theatre*, Oxford/Providence, Berg, 1994, p. 9, n. 5; A. Hallamore Caesar, *Characters and Authors in Luigi Pirandello*, Oxford, Clarendon, 1998, p. 244.

18. D. Bini, 'Pirandello's Philosophy and Philosophers', in *A Companion to Pirandello Studies*, ed. J. L. DiGaetani , New York etc., Greenwood Press, 1991, p. 17.

19. *SPSV*, pp. 900; 896.

20. The 'Preface' is published in: L. Pirandello, *Maschere Nude*, II, ed. A. D'Amico, Milan, Mondadori, ser. 'I Meridiani', 1993, pp. 653–667; Felicity Firth has translated the 'Preface' ('Introduction') into English, see: L. Pirandello, *Collected Plays,* ed. R. Rietty, Vol. 2, London and New York, Calder and Riverrun Press, 1988, xi–xxv.

21. *Allegre*. IV, in *SPSV*, p. 461.

22. The essays are: *Da lontano; Feminismo* [*sic*]; *Ricomincio a veder l'Europa*, now in *SPSV*, pp. 1064–1075. The articles are: *Una spazzola!; I filatori*, now in *SPSV*, pp. 1060–1063.

23. Now in: L.Pirandello, *Novelle per un anno*, II, ii, ed. M. Costanzo, Milan, Mondadori, ser. 'I Meridiani', 1987, p. 788.

24. R.D. Laing, *The Divided Self*, London etc., Penguin (Pelican edition), 1969 (first published1959). The quotations are taken, respectively, from pp. 91 and 80.

25. This essay is published in *SPSV*, pp. 181–206.

26. F. Firth, 'Freedom and Fragmentation: the Excluded Woman' in *Luigi Pirandello: the Theatre of Paradox*, cit., pp. 173–185.

27. Now in: L. Pirandello, *Tutti i romanzi,* I, ed. G. Macchia, M. Costanzo, Milan, Mondadori, ser. 'I Meridiani', 1986 (7th ed.), p. 580. The translation is mine.

28. R. Luperini, 'Allegorismo versus Simbolismo', in *Pirandello e D'Annunzio*, ed. E. Lauretta, Palermo, Palumbo, 1989, p. 112.

29. The essay can be found in *SPSV*, pp. 1015–1018; there is an English translation in *Luigi Pirandello in the Theatre*, cit., pp. 20–23.

30. E. Kris, *Psychoanalytic Explorations in Art*, London, Allen & Unwin, 1953, p. 194.

31. D. Lodge, *The Modes of Modern Writing*, London, Melbourne, Auckland, Edward Arnold, 1977 (paperback 1979), p. 40.

32. On Berecche's Don-Quixote-like 'vocation' see P. Milone, '"Un'altra vita"? Pirandello, la guerra e l'arte' in *Pirandello e la politica*, ed. E. Lauretta, Milan, Mursia, 1992, pp. 109–160.

33. G. D'Annunzio, *Per la più grande Italia*, in *Prose di ricerca*, vol. I, Milan, Mondadori, 4th. ed., 1966, p. 40 (my translation).

34. G. Giudice, *Luigi Pirandello*, cit., p. 268 (my translation).

35. The interview was for 'Noi e il mondo', v, No. 4, 1 April 1915.

36. See in particular Freud's essay *Creative Writers and Day-dreaming*, of 1907 (published in 1908), now in *S. Freud, Art and Literature*, The Penguin Freud Library, vol 14, London, Penguin, 1990, pp. 129–141.

37. P. de Man, *Allegories of Reading*, New Haven and London, Yale University Press, 1979 p. 49.

23

AUTHOR'S NOTE
TO THE 1934 EDITION

I'm placing *Berecche and the War*, a story in eight chapters written in the months preceding our entry into the World War, in this the XIVth volume of my collected *Stories for a Year*. It reflects the case I witnessed, with astonishment to begin with and almost laughingly, then with compassion, of a studious man educated like so many others at that time in the German fashion, and especially in the disciplines of history and philology. During the long period of our alliance Germany had, for such people, become not just spiritually but also in their thoughts and feelings, as an intimate part of their lives, their ideal native land. As our intervention against her, called for by the most vital and sound part of the Italian people and then accepted by the whole nation, became imminent, they therefore felt, as it were, lost; and, compelled in the end by the very force of events to take back their true native land to themselves, they suffered a crisis which, from this aspect, seemed to me to be worthy of representation.

BERECCHE AND THE WAR

I

THE BEER-HOUSE

Outside, another hot and sunny day. Southern streets beneath the burning blue of the sky, scored by harsh violet-purple shadows. And people are walking there, light and airy yet bursting with life and colour. Voices in the sun and cobbles ringing underfoot

Inside, the good expatriate German has recreated a bit of his native land around him, between the four wood-panelled walls of his beer-house; and he breathes in its air in the stench of the barrels coming from the cellar next door, in the fatty smell of the *würstel* piled up on the counter, in the pungent smell of the boxes of appetizing spices, all labelled in stiff, upright German letters. They're there as well, those cherished German letters of his – larger, stiffer, more upright – in the shiny, brightly-coloured deep-blue, yellow and red posters hanging on the walls. And the tankards, the *krügel* decorated with figures, the beer-mugs, set out in orderly fashion on the shelves, act as sentinels guarding his illusion.[1]

What faraway, anguished voice, from time to time, when the beer-house is empty and dark, sings deep in his heart the song:

Nur in Deutschland, nur in Deutschland
Da will ich sterben ... ?[2]

With his large, tawny-red face assuming a wide, friendly smile, until yesterday he greeted his faithful Roman customers with welcoming guttural sounds. Now he stands frowning and still behind his counter and no longer greets anyone.

Always the first to arrive at the beer-house, Berecche, much concerned, watches him from the little table at the back of the room, with his worthy *krügel* in front of him. Concerned as he is, his face is grim, because his situation, too, has all of a sudden become difficult.

Up to a few days ago Federico Berecche made much of his German origins, clearly apparent from his square physique, reddish hair and light blue eyes but also from his surname, Berecche, a corrupt pronunciation, in his view, of a typically German name.[3] And he was proud of all the benefits Italy had gained from her long alliance with what were

29

then the Central Powers, not to mention the outstanding virtues of the Germanic peoples which he, for so many years had striven rigorously to put into practice, both in himself and in the ordering of his life and his household; above all else method. Method, method.

In that beer-house, on the marble top of a small table, they have drawn a caricature of him: a chess-board with Berecche walking over it, goose-stepping like a German foot-soldier and a pointed helmet, with a spike, on his large head.

The essence of the caricature is in the chess-board: meant to show that Berecche sees the world like that, in squares, and walks through it in the German way with a deliberate, measured tread like an honest pawn dependant on the king, the castles and the knights.

Under the caricature some wag has written: *MiddleAges*, with a big exclamation mark.

"Germany, back in the MiddleAges?" Federico Berecche asked indignantly when he saw that drawing on the marble table top, not recognising himself, of course, in the caricature but recognising the spiked German helmet. "Back in the MiddleAges, Germany? Come on! My dear friends! Way, way ahead in culture, in industry, in music and the most fearsome army in the world."

As proof of which, taking his deep-blue and yellow wooden box out of his pocket he had lit his pipe with a *streichholz*,[4] as Berecche despises the use of Italian wax matches as soft.

So when the first announcement was made of Italy's declaration of neutrality in the European conflict he felt a spurt of anger against the Italian Government.[5]

"What about the pact of alliance? Is Italy withdrawing? And from now on who will ever be able to trust Italy again? Neutral? So is this the moment to stand idly at the window while everyone is mobilizing? You have to make your position clear straightaway, for heaven's sake! And our position is ..."

They didn't let him finish. A chorus of vehement protests, of abuse and insults rained down on him from all sides and overwhelmed him. "The pact of alliance? After Austria has torn it up by her offensive? after Germany's gone mad, declaring war to the right, war to the left, war right up to the stars, without letting us know, completely ignoring our situation?[6] Idiot! Imbecile! A fine way to keep your word! Fight against our own interests? Help Austria to win? Us? And what about our unredeemed lands?[7] And our coasts and islands, with the British and French fleets against us? Can we be against Britain? Idiot! Imbecile!"

To begin with Federico Berecche tried to stand up to them, retaliating by reminding his furious opponents of the wrongs and insults they had suffered at the hands of France.

"Tunis! Have you forgotten so soon about the reason for the Triple Alliance?[8] And just recently, during the Libyan war, the way they smuggled supplies to the Turks?[9] And tomorrow – and you're the idiots and imbeciles – tomorrow we'll find ourselves at Campoformio or Villafranca again!"[10]

Then, interrupted at almost every word, he tried to show that in any case ... "Well, allow me to say ... we're neutral? But we can't be! In name only! Because in fact could there be a more hostile act than this? It's an inestimable advantage, especially for France. You're just like sheep ... neutrality ... What about Niccolò Machiavelli ... (they had the audacity to call him, a retired teacher of history, an idiot), yes, Machiavelli, Machiavelli, on the dangers of neutrality, the great dilemma: *If two powerful neighbouring states of yours come to blows ...*"[11]

A general howl of disapproval cut short his quotation. But since he himself said it was neutrality in name only, how did Machiavelli and his dilemma come into it? A hostile act, yes indeed! Against Austria, yes indeed! Because Austria is harming our interests. To the point where she took action without letting us know. And we should thank our lucky stars, because she's released us from our obligation by her own rash behaviour. And you talk about tomorrow? Do you think that France and Russia, when they win, will ignore the advantages they've gained from us staying out? Oh, come on, Britain will take care of us, because in her own interests she can't allow our power in the Mediteranean to shrink.

With these and similar arguments Italy's neutrality was defended; with such heat that, in the end, Berecche had to give up and didn't dare open his mouth again. The idea that Italy's geographical position will tomorrow allow her to steer the course of events made a deep impression on him. Steer the course of events! That means that fortune will shift in whichever direction we, at the opportune moment, choose. And there can be no doubt as to the right direction.

"Well at least let's arm ourselves, for goodness' sake!" Berecche boomed out, exasperated, raising his hairy fists.

And as he shouted, at the cry "there's no point" Federico Berecche felt himself, in the depths of his heart, to be German.

However, yesterday evening at the beer-house he no longer dared defend the Germans against the terrible accusations of his friends. Not a single one of them, not even good, sleepy old Fongi, who always agreed with him for the sake of peace and quiet, supported Germany.

Good old Fongi said nothing, but from time to time turned to look at him fearfully out of the corner of his eye, perhaps expecting a rebellious outburst from him at any moment. And Berecche was almost tempted to give him a punch in the face. He began to breathe again when his friends moved on from talking about the Germans to more general considerations. One of these particularly impressed itself on him, also because of the sad and serious way his friend opposite, in a moment of silence, pronounced it, looking at the spittle-like foam left by the froth on top of the beer inside his little beer-mug.

"In the end, however terrible the events and dreadful the consequences we can at least be glad of this: that it has been our fate to witness the dawn of another life. We've lived for forty, fifty, even sixty years with the feeling that things couldn't go on as they were; that the stresses and strains were gradually becoming more intense, and we'd reach breaking-point; that in the end there'd be a war. And now it's here. Dreadful. But at least we're seeing it. The anxieties, the hardships, the torment and the longings of such a long and unbearable wait will come to an end and find a release. And we shall see the great tomorrow. Because everything will necessarily change, and we'll all certainly come out of this terrifying upheaval completely transformed."

At once Berecche's gaze fell on a little table and three chairs in the room which the customers were just getting up to leave. He stared at them for a long time, feeling more and more and with each passing moment a strange, melancholic envy for those three empty chairs and that deserted table.

He turned away from them with a deep sigh when another of his friends began to say:

"And who knows! Just think that there were once great world civilizations in India, China, Persia, Egypt, Greece and Rome. A light is lit and shines for many centuries in one region, in one continent; then, little by little, it dies down, flickers and goes out. Who knows! Perhaps it will now be Europe's turn. Who can foresee the consequences of such an unprecedented conflict? Perhaps no-one will win and everything – wealth, industry, civilization – will be destroyed. Perhaps the next great civilization will start in the Americas, while our ruin will gradually become complete and the time will come when ships will land on the shores of Europe as you would if you came as conquerors."

Heaving another and deeper sigh Berecche saw himself far, far away with the whole of Europe, thrust back into the obscurity of a fabled prehistoric age. Shortly afterwards he got to his feet and brusquely took leave of his friends to go home.

II

IN THE EVENING, ON THE WAY HOME

Berecche lives in an isolated side-road at the end of via Nomentana.[12]
On the left, in that side-road, which is barely marked out and still without street lamps, there are just three recently-built houses; on the right is a country hedge surrounding plots of land still to be sold and from where, on the moist evening air, comes a fresh smell of new-mown hay.

It's just as well that one of the three houses has been bought by a very rich old prelate who lives there with three nieces, withered spinsters who, as dusk is falling, take it in turns to mount a portable ladder to light a little lamp in front of the small blue and white porcelain figure of the Madonna, placed about a month ago at one corner of the house.

At night that merciful little lamp shines in the darkness of the lonely road.

Living there is like being in the countryside; and just as in the open countryside you can hear in the silence the night trains roaring along in the distance. Behind the gate of the houses the dogs hurl themselves forward, barking furiously every time they hear footsteps. But at least Berecche can enjoy a bit of open countryside in front, and the peace and quiet.

From the four groundfloor windows, in a wide expanse of sky, he can see the stars, which he talks to at length during his leisurely evenings as a peaceful pensioner. The stars and the moon, when there is one. And beneath the moon, the pine-trees and cypresses of Villa Torlonia.[13] He has a little bit of garden as well, for his exclusive use, with a tiny fountain, whose gurgling in the silence of the night is dear to him.

But, alas, his wife, the two daughters who still live with him and his only son, already an Arts student at the University, his servant and now, as well, the elder daughter's fiancé feel nothing of the poetry of the solitude, the starry sky and the moon above the cypresses and pines in the patrician villa, and they heave great sighs or yawn plaintively like hungry dogs at the monotonous, endless gurgling of that delightful little fountain. It seems to them that they're banished, in exile. But Berecche – method, method, method – holds firm, and has renewed the lease for three years.

Now, the deeper he plunges into the darkness of the isolated, deserted street beneath the fourfold row of big, motionless trees the heavier the nightmare of the general destruction which will extinguish every light of science and civilization in the old continent of Europe weighs down on his spirit.

What kind of new life will it be when the terrible chaos has subsided into its ruins? How will he, at fifty-three years of age, come out of it completely transformed?

There will be other needs, other hopes, other thoughts and other feelings. Everything will inevitably change. But not, for all that, these big trees which have the good fortune neither to think nor to feel! When humanity all around them has changed they will still be the same trees, just as they are now.

And alas Federico Berecche is very much afraid that it's now far too late for him, as well, to change, deep down, whatever happens during the time still remaining to him. He's grown used to conversing with the stars, every night; and under their cold light all earthly feelings have, as it were, become rarefied within him. You wouldn't think so, because on the outside his will to live in that particular, methodical, German way of his is still clearly and stubbornly apparent. But deep down he is tired and sad, with a sadness that is unlikely to be affected by what is happening in the world outside.

Let the French, the Russians and the British win, or the Germans and the Austrians; let Italy, too, be dragged into the war or not, and let there be the hardships and gloom of defeat or let victory triumph frenetically in all the towns of the peninsula; let the map of Europe be changed; what will never change – and this is certain – is the animosity, the deep rancour his wife feels against him, and his regret at reaching the evening of his life without a single memory of any real joy. And no power on earth or in heaven can restore sight to the eyes of his youngest daughter, who has been blind for six years.

Now, when he goes back into the house, he will find her still sitting in one corner of the little dining room, with her wax-like hands on her legs and her little blond head leaning against the wall, and since from her sightless face it's impossible to tell if she is asleep or awake he will ask her, as every evening:

"Are you asleep, Ghetina?"[14]

And Margheritina, without moving her head from the wall, will reply: "No, papa, I'm not asleep ..."

She never speaks, she never complains, she seems to be asleep all the time; perhaps she never sleeps.

Continuing on his way under the big trees Berecche clears his throat, because as a strong man brought up in the German fashion he doesn't want to choke with distress. But everyone lives in the light; he himself lives in the light and can resign himself to his fate, while instead there's this horrible thing in life: that his daughter lives in the darkness, always, and stays there, in silence, with her little head leaning on the wall, waiting to die; and who knows how long that wait will last.

Another life: other thoughts, other feelings. Yes, that's right! Carlotta, his eldest daughter, stopped going to university a year ago because she got engaged to a fine boy from the Val di Non in the Trentino who'd graduated just a year earlier in literature and philosophy from the University of Rome; a fine boy, with plenty of spirit and noble sentiments and full of good intentions: but still without a position in life; and now, more than ever, uncertain about his future. Three of his brothers, at San Zeno, have been called up. His father is the mayor of San Zeno. So those three poor brothers of his weren't able to escape from the hateful obligation to fight for Austria, and who knows, if things go badly for us, perhaps, tomorrow, against Italy as well. What a terrible thing! He, in the meantime, didn't report when he was called up, and so it's goodbye to the Valle di Non, goodbye to San Zeno, goodbye to his old parents: as a deserter in time of war he would tomorrow, if captured, be hanged or shot in the back. But he hopes that Italy … who knows! He would rush off and volunteer, even at the cost of finding himself fighting against those poor brothers of his. He would rush off, together with Faustino.[15]

Berecche starts to clear his throat again even harder, so that he nearly tears it, at the thought that Faustino, his only son, his favourite child, who fortunately this year isn't old enough to be called up, might go and enlist as a volunteer together with his future brother-in-law. He couldn't any longer forbid him to do it; but by God – damn his throat! damn the damp evening! – even though he is a good fifty-three years old, and with all that flesh which has come to weigh him down, he too would then go and enlist, so as not to let Faustino go alone, so as not to die of terror once a day whenever there was news of the fighting, knowing that Faustino was under fire; yes indeed, he, Berecche, with his great paunch, would volunteer as well even … even against the Germans, yes he would!

And yes … there it was already, straightaway, the other life. War, with his young son on one side and, on the other, his other, new son, going to conquer the unredeemed lands. Who knows? It might happen tomorrow.

Berecche has arrived; he turns right; he goes into the lonely side-road. There in the thick dark is the little red light in front of the Madonna. Miracles of the *other life*. Berecche stops in front of that light; he takes off his hat, unseen by anyone, to say something to that little Madonna.

And let the dogs carry on barking furiously behind the gates, if they want to.

III

THE WAR ON THE MAP

Berecche remembers. Forty-four years ago.[16] Little French flags and little Prussian flags – only those at that time – fixed as now with pins onto
the map spread out on a small table in the dining room. *The theatre of
war*. What a lovely game for him, then a boy of nine!

As if in a dream he sees again that yellow dining room in his
father's house, with the brass oil lamps and the green silk lampshades;
lots of chests all around draped in flowery covers; over here a bow-
fronted chest of drawers, over there a bracket and in the corners two
sets of shelves, with baskets of coloured marble fruit and wax flowers
on the different levels; on the shelves to the left a little porcelain clock
in the shape of windmill, which he particularly loved, with one sail
broken.[17]

Around that little table which, the only decrepit survivor, is now, hidden by a new cover, in his son's bedroom, he sees his father and some
friends discussing the Franco-Prussian War. Ill-fitting jackets buttoned
right up to the neck and wide, straight-legged trousers. Waxed mous-
taches and a tuft of hair on the lower lip like Napoleon III or beards
running under their chin from ear to ear like Cavour.[18] Bending over
that map they were tracing the routes taken by the armies with their
fingers, according to the information and forecasts in the few, out-of-
date newspapers of that time, and they talked excitedly and no-one
allowed the finger of one of the others to linger peacefully on any particular trail. Another finger came along, and then another and another:
everyone wanted to put in his own. And each of those fingers – he
remembers – straightaway, to his childish eyes, took on a strange personality: one of them, squat and stubborn, stayed obstinately put in one
place; another, wiry and insolent, stood in front of it quivering with the
desire to move on from that same point; and now a third, a crooked little finger, came up stealthily to help one of the others, and crept in
between those two which drew aside to let it pass. And what cries, what
snorts of impatience, what exclamations or strident peals of laughter
over all those fingers, amidst a cloud of smoke! From time to time, a
name rang out like a cannon-shot:

"MacMahon!"[19]

36

Berecche smiles at the distant memory, then frowns and sits intent, knees wide with his clenched fists resting on them. He contemplates the map which is in front of him, now, with so many little flags in so many colours. If the little nine-year-old boy who had then played at war could come alive out of his memory, there in his study, in front of himself grown old, goodness knows how he would enjoy himself playing the new, bigger, more varied and complicated game with all those gaily-coloured little flags! Belgium, France and Britain over here, against Germany; and Russia against Germany over there in Eastern Prussia and Poland;[20] Serbia and Montenegro down there against Austria; and, still against Austria, Russia, further up, in Galicia.

What an irresistible urge the little nine-year-old boy would feel to make those little German flags speed along, flying over Belgium among the bowing and scraping of the little Belgian flags; take them to Paris in a few leaps and bounds; plant a couple of them there victoriously and then, in a few more leaps and bounds, send them back and hurl them against Russia alongside the Austrian ones!

And it's that – incredibly – just what he as a little nine-year-old boy would have done in the game that the Germans thought they could now do in earnest, after forty-four years of military preparation! They really thought that neutral Belgium would tranquilly let itself be invaded and let them through without putting up the least resistance, at Liège or Namur, so as to give France, as yet unprepared, time to gather its armies and Britain to land its first auxiliary troops: just that!

Every evening his friends at the beer-house denounce the iniquity of the invasion and the acts of barbarous cruelty at the top of their voices; as for himself, Berecche doesn't protest, he remains silent, even though consumed with anger within, because he can't shout at them to their faces as he would like to:

"Imbeciles! It's no use screaming and shouting! It's war!"

He doesn't protest, and he swallows his anger, because he is shaken. Shaken not by the invasion, not by the acts of ferocity but by the colossal bestiality of the Germans. Shaken to the core.

From the heights of his love and admiration for Germany, which had grown out of all proportion over the years, this colossal bestiality has come crashing down like an avalanche to smash all he had: everything he believed in, the world as he had little by little constructed it for himself from the time he was nine years old, in the German way, with method, with discipline in everything: in his studies, in his life, in his habits of mind and body.

Oh, what a disaster! The nine-year-old boy had grown up, yes he had; it was all he had loved, all he had admired; and it had become a florid, prosperous giant who knew everything better than anyone else, who did everything better than anyone else, and now after forty-four years of preparation had turned out to be a brute beast: brawny, indeed, with well-drilled and powerful hands and hind legs; but which seriously thought it was still possible to play at war like a naughty, savage little nine-year old boy, or as if it were alone in the world and everyone else counted for nothing: crossing Belgium in leaps and bounds and going to plant the little flags, a couple of them, on Paris, and then away again at great speed, in a few more leaps and bounds, to plant them on Petersburg and Moscow. And Britain?

"Incredible! Incredible!"

Shaken as he is Berecche keeps on exclaiming like this, he can't find anything else to say:

"Incredible!"

And he scratches his head with both hands and breathes out heavily, and some of the little flags fly away, some bend and others fall over onto the map.

Shut away there in his study, so that no-one can see him, Berecche feels his heart rebel at the memory of what he meant by German method, when he was a student, at the memory of the inexpressible satisfaction it brought him when, with his eyes tired by his laborious, patient interpretation of the texts and documents, but with his conscience at rest and certain of having taken everything into account, of not having overlooked anything, of not having neglected any useful and necessary piece of research, his hands lingered, in the evening, on returning home from the libraries, on the wealth of information there on his little study table, contained in his voluminous card-indexes. And he feels his heart bleed all the more because he is now aware, with a dull resentment, that because of the satisfaction he derived from that method, deep down he was cowardly enough to ignore a certain voice of his reason secretly rebelling against some German assertions which not only offended his sense of logic but also, in his heart of hearts, his latin sentiment: the assertion, for example, that the Romans had no gift for poetry; and, alongside this assertion, the demonstration that the whole early history of Rome was a legend. Now, it could only be one or the other. If that history was a legend, that is fiction, how could they deny the gift of poetry? Either poetry or history. Impossible to deny both at the same time. Either true history, and great; or poetry, no less great and true. And at this point he remembers what Goethe,[21] in his old age, said after reading the first two volumes of Niebuhr's *History of Rome*,[22] up to the first Punic war:

"Up to now, we believed in the greatness of a Lucretia, of a Mucius Scaevola;[23] why should we destroy the greatness of such figures with our petty arguments? If the Romans were great enough to believe they were capable of such things, should we not at least be great enough to credit what they say?'

Goethe, Schiller, and first Lessing and then Kant, Hegel[24] ... Oh all these giants, when Germany was small, when she was not yet Germany! And now she is a giant, and has flung herself belly down on the ground, hands clasped under her chest, with one elbow here, on Belgium and in France and the other there, on Russia and in Poland:

"Move me, if you can!"

For how long will the brute beast hold out in that position?

"Oh, brute beast, there are so very many of them! And you thought you could settle it all with two blows of your paws! You were wrong! You saw nothing; you didn't have a quick victory; you flung yourself down like that on the ground, with your elbows out on both sides; can you hold out for long? one day soon they'll move you, they'll dismember you, they'll tear you to pieces!"

Berecche jumps to his feet, flushed and panting, as if he had made the supreme effort to shift the brute beast from where it lay.

IV

THE WAR IN THE FAMILY

What's happening in there?

Screams and sounds of weeping in the dining-room. Berecche comes running; there he finds his elder daughter's fiancé, Dr Gino Viesi from the Valle di Non in the Trentino, pale, with his eyes full of tears and a letter in his hand.

"News?"

"His brothers!" shouts Carlotta, trembling with rage and staring at him, her eyes red with weeping but accusing.

Gino Viesi, without looking at him, shows him the letter in his trembling hand.

Two of his three brothers, 35-year-old Filippo, father of four children, and 26-year-old Erminio, married a few days ago had been called up by Austria and sent to Galicia ... "What's happened?" No-one replies.

"Both of them? Dead?"

The young man, racked by a fresh outburst of sobbing, makes a sign – one – with one finger, before hiding his face.

"One of them, certainly" Berecche's wife says to him in a low voice, with hatred, venom even, in it. Carlotta gets up to comfort her fiancé and to weep with him.

"Erminio?"

His wife, harsh, stocky and dishevelled shakes her head: no.

"The other one? the one with four children?"

Gino Viesi begins to sob even louder on Carlotta's shoulder.

"And Erminio?"

Irritated, his wife says :

"No-one knows: he's reported missing!"

Margherita, the little blind girl, doesn't have eyes to see how the others are weeping, what they look like (she doesn't even know what one face, that of Gino, her sister's fiancé, whom she too calls Gino, is like), she doesn't have eyes to see, no, but she still has eyes to weep with; and she weeps in silence, tears that she doesn't see, that no-one sees, over there, set apart, in her little corner.

"And not one of you is speaking up for us!" Gino Viesi finally bursts out, raising his head from Carlotta's shoulder and coming towards

Berecche. "Not one of you is speaking up for us! No-one's doing anything! They've sent all the men from the Trentino and Trieste to the slaughter! And down here you all know that we feel exactly the same as you do; and that up there they're waiting for you, as you well know! But right now not one of you is personally affected by the torment we feel when we see our brothers being forced to violate those feelings we all share and sent to the slaughter up there! Not a single one of you ... And those few of us here from Trento and Trieste are like exiles in our own country; and it's a miracle that a loyalist like you isn't shouting at me that my real place is there, fighting and dying for Austria with my other brothers!"

"Me?" exclaims Berecche, in amazement.

"You, all of you!" the young man goes on in his rage and grief. "I've seen you, I've heard you; you don't care at all; you say it isn't worth Italy's while to bestir herself to take Trento, as probably Austria will let her have it without a fight, one day, or to take Trieste, *which doesn't want to be Italian* ... Isn't that what you say? That's what you say and that's what you think! And that's why you've let us be trampled on, always; and you've never been able to achieve anything for us at all!"

Gino Viesi is young and grief-stricken; and so, with his handsome face ablaze and his lovely blond locks in disarray, he cannot understand that nothing is quite so irritating, at certain times, as hearing someone put forward and state out loud feelings we secretly share, but which we want to keep well hidden, stifling them so we can maintain a position which has already shown itself to be false; at such times we flare up in defence of our position, and against the feelings we share but see held up as the opposite of ours, and we see ourselves drawn into upholding what, fundamentally, we consider to be false and unjust.

This is what happens now to Berecche. Angrily he shouts at the young man:

"What would you like us to do? Should Italy prevent Austria, when she's at war, from sending the men of Trento and Trieste against Russia and Serbia? As long as you're under her control, she's within her rights!"

"Oh really! you're talking about rights?" shouts Gino Viesi in turn. "And so, if this is Austria's legitimate right what am I doing, according to you? Am I failing in my duty by staying here? We should all go and die for Austria, shouldn't we? Go on, say it! Of course it's her right ... that of the master who whips his slaves into going wherever he wants! But who has ever recognised Austria's right to control Trento, Trieste, Istria and Dalmatia?[25] Austria herself knows that she doesn't have the right! To the point where she's doing everything to suppress us, to blot out all traces of Italian culture and identity from our regions! Austria does know it; and you don't, you who let her do as she likes! And now, in the face of a war which right away, from the very beginning, was obviously harmful to us, against our interests, it was right to decide on neutrality, wasn't it, and not on arming yourselves to liberate us and to defend our interests right there where Austria first began to threaten them?"

"But neutrality ..." Berecche ventures to say.

Gino Viesi doesn't give him time to continue: "Yes, it's all very well for you" he goes on. "Because no-one could come here and force you to march and fight against your beliefs and interests! But have you thought about us, up there, who should be what your beliefs are all about, who are exactly where what you call 'your interests' lie? By being neutral you've let us from up there be taken and dragged to the slaughter; and you still say that this was Austria's right; and no-one cries out for revenge for the blood of my dead brothers! They all shout instead: *Long live Belgium! Long live France!* Just now, on my way here, I met the columns of demonstrators on the streets of Rome. All feverish with excitement!"

"And Faustino?" Berecche asks all of a sudden, turning to his wife.

"He's with the demonstrators as well!" Gino Viesi replies at once. "*Long live Belgium! Long live France!*"

In a fury Berecche points his finger, threateningly, at his wife:

"And you've let him leave the house? And you didn't say a thing to me about it? Don't I count for anything any longer? Is that how my ideas and feelings are respected now? I'm telling you and I'm telling everybody! So that's it? *Long live Belgium, long live France...* Well then I want to see what France will do, tomorrow, when she's won with other people's help! Tomorrow the cockerel will turn on us again, when it has raised its victorious crest once more, with other people's help ... Fools! fools! fools!"

And after this outburst Berecche rushes off to shut himself in his study again, deeply upset and trembling at the effort he has had to make to control himself.

Oh what a terrible business ... oh God, what a terrible business ...

Everything within him has collapsed. But can he really allow the others to see that? Germany, until yesterday, was the source of his prestige, of his authority at home; it was everything to him, Germany was, until yesterday. And now ... this is how it is: now every morning – to cap it all – as soon as the servant returns from doing the daily shopping his wife rounds on him, demanding that he justify all the increases in food prices – so much on bread, so much on meat, so much on eggs – as if he had wanted, as if he had started, the war! Stricken to the heart and with his beliefs shattered, he also finds himself being deluged by the flood of trivia coming from his wife, and it's a miracle she doesn't hold him responsible as well for the danger Faustino runs of being called up early and sent to fight, if Italy, too, is dragged into the war! Isn't he the one who represents Germany at home; Germany, that wanted the war?

And yes indeed, for the sake of his prestige in the family, he has to carry on representing Germany, if not ... If not, what? This is what it has come to: his son slips out of the house and goes to shout *Long live France* through the streets of Rome with the other imbeciles; and that other poor boy in there, two of whose brothers have been killed, holds him responsible for Italy's neutrality and for the slaughter of the men from the Trentino and Trieste over by Lemberg![26]

Oh, how infamous Germany is! She didn't even begin to foresee the harm she was doing, the tragedy she was causing for the multitudes who, in Italy and in other countries too, with such great effort and bitter sacrifices, stifling so many yawns, gulping down so much indigestible stuff, erudition, music, philosophy, had learnt to love Germany and to make a profession of this love! Infamous Germany, so this is how she now repays her victims for the love and admiration they've professed for her for so many years!

Powerless to do anything else, Berecche would like to stab her over and over again, in secret, on the map, with the pins of all the little French, British, Belgian, Russian, Serbian and Montenegran flags!

V

THE WAR IN THE WORLD

Evening has come. But he stays in his study in the dark and paces around with one hand over his mouth, looking from time to time at the last glow of the twilight in the panes of the two windows. From one of them he sees the little red lamp, already lit, of the little Madonna of the house opposite; he knits his brows and goes over to the window.

Then, in the light of the big lamp which shines into the hall, he sees his wife, holding Margheritina by the hand, leave the house and cross the garden.

You wouldn't guess from her walk, dear little thing. You almost wouldn't guess, if you didn't know. At least seeing her like that, from behind. Perhaps because she trusts the hand that guides her. Only, if you look closely at her, she holds her small head a bit stiffly on her neck and her thin little shoulders a bit hunched. The gravel doesn't crunch under her little feet, because her whole being is striving upwards to avoid touching what she can't see, and her tiny body weighs almost nothing.

But where is she going with her mother at this time of night? And how is it that Faustino hasn't come home yet? Has Gino Viesi left?

Berecche goes to put all these questions to Carlotta. There's no-one left in the dining room. Carlotta has shut herself away in her room and in the dark, like him, is still weeping; she replies to the questions in the same curt, rude tone as her mother: "Gino? He's gone." "Faustino? How should she know?" "Mummy? Gone with Ghetina to Monsignor's house for the novena."

For the last three nights, in Monsignor's house opposite, they've been saying prayers for the Pope who is ill, for the Pope who is dying.[27]

Berecche goes back into his study, goes over to the window again and looks at the house opposite, saddened now and full of grief for this Pope, a holy old peasant, made worthy of his great office only though the complete sincerity of his faith. Oh, who more than he, truly pious like his name, wanted to call Christ back into the hearts of the faithful? And he's dying as the war rages around him, dying of grief because of the war. Certainly he, on his deathbed, won't say, as some close to him are perhaps quietly saying, that this war, for France, is God's just retribution for the wrongs she has done to the Church. For him those others who have dared to call on God to protect the progress and the carnage of their armies, and who have dared to see and extol the sign of divine protection in the victories which have come from their acts of atrocity, are certainly far more iniquitous sinners. He hasn't said another word; horrified, he has withdrawn that hand that some wanted him to raise to bless this monstrous wickedness; and he has shut himself up in the grief which is killing him.

Damned light of reason! Damned reason that is unable to blind itself with faith! By its light he, Berecche, sees, or believes he sees, so many things that now prevent him from praying with his little daughter Margherita, blind in her blind faith, for the good Pope who is dying. But he is glad, yes he is, that his Margheritina is praying over there; he is glad that one part of him, so painfully loved, which does not have his light of reason, should blindly pray over there for the good Pope who is dying. It really seems to him that, with the pale, delicate hands of his little blind daughter joined in prayer, he, from his soul which itself is unable to pray, is giving something now – what he can – in intercession for the good Pope who's dying.

In the meantime eight o'clock in the evening comes, then nine; then ten, and Faustino still hasn't come home.

His mother, who came back some time ago with Ghetina from Monsignor's house, and his sister, Carlotta, have come into the study several times to express their dismay, to beseech him with hands clasped to do something, to go and look for him, so that at least they'll know, which God forbid, that something terrible hasn't happened to him during those accursed demonstrations.

Berecche drove them out in a rage, and shouted at them point blank that he wouldn't do anything because he doesn't care at all any more about that young scoundrel, no longer considers him to be his son, and if he's been trampled to the ground, wounded or arrested that's absolutely fine by him.

Finally, a little after half past ten, Faustino comes home, in fear and trembling at the thought of his father but still enraged and full of what has happened to him. He's been arrested. But he is quivering with indignation and disgust at the anger of the soldiers, fortunately just a small group, who arrested him, manhandling him and shouting at him:

"You coward, you're doing this because tomorrow you don't have to go and fight!"

And now all that he wants to do is to go and fight, so as to reply in the only way possible to those soldiers who arrested him.

"Be quiet!" his mother shouts at him, more dishevelled than ever. "If

45

your father in there should hear you!"

But Berecche doesn't move from his study. He doesn't want to see him. When his wife comes to tell him that he has come back, he orders her to tell him not to dare show his face. A little later, Carlotta puts her head round the door:

"Supper is ready. Fausto's in his room."

"I'm staying here! Tell the maid to bring me my supper in here. I don't want to see anyone."

But he can't eat. He has a lump in his throat more from rage than from anguish. Little by little, however, he begins to calm down and to fall, almost, into a deep sense of oblivion and detachment which is very familiar to him. It is his philosophical mood which gradually, as evening falls, regains the ascendant over him.

Berecche gets up, goes over to the nearest window, sits down and starts to look at the stars.

He sees this little planet Earth in endless space, as perhaps none or maybe just one of those stars can see it, going on and on, for no known purpose, in that space whose end is unknown. It goes on, the basest of specks of dust, a tiny drop of black water, and the wind, as it speeds along, cancels out the lights marking the places where men live, in that very small part where the speck is not liquid, turning them into a violent, faintly glimmering blur. If in the heavens they knew that in that faintly glimmering blur there are millions and millions of restless beings, who seriously think that from that little speck of dust they can lay down the law to the whole universe, impose their way of thinking and feeling on it, and their God, the little God created by their tiny little souls and whom they believe has created those heavens and all those stars; and there they are, taking him, this God who has created the heavens and all the stars and worshipping him, and clothing him in their fashion and asking him to take account of all their small afflictions and to protect them even in their sorriest doings, in their stupid wars. If in the heavens they knew that, in this hour of time which has no end, these millions and millions of imperceptible beings, in this faintly glimmering blur, are all involved in a furious brawl for reasons which they believe to be supremely important for their existence, and which the heavens, the stars, the God who has created these heavens and all these stars, should all concern themselves with minute by minute, committed to the hilt on one side or the other. Are there some who believe there is no time in the heavens? That everything is swallowed up and disappears in this dark, endless void? And that on this very same speck, tomorrow, in a thousand years, nothing will remain or scarcely a thing will be said of this war which now seems so appalling and dreadful to us?

46

Berecche remembers how, just a few years ago, he taught history to his secondary-school pupils: *Around 950, after the Danes who had rebelled against him had been reduced to obedience, Otto went into Bohemia to fight Duke Boleslas, who had made himself independent, and pushing on as far as Prague he forced that Duke to become a vassal of the German kingdom again. At the same time his brother Henry went out to fight the Hungarians and drove them beyond the Theiss, taking from them the lands they had conquered during the reign of Louis the Child ...* [28]

Tomorrow, in a thousand years, another Berecche, a teacher of history, will tell his pupils that around 1914 there were, still powerful and flourishing, two empires in the centre of Europe; one called the German Empire, on whose throne sat a certain Wilhelm II of a dynasty which has now disappeared and which was apparently called Hohenzollern; and the other called the Austrian Empire, on whose throne sat a certain very old Franz Joseph of the Habsburg dynasty.[29] These two Emperors were allies, and both, or so at least certain facts seem to indicate, although this does not seem very probable in the light of logic, also allies of the King of Italy, a certain Victor Emanuel III[30] of the dynasty of Savoy, who, however, at least at the outset did not join in the war which that German Emperor, taking – it appears – as his pretext the assassination of someone called Franz Ferdinand, hereditary Archduke of Austria, by the Serbs, stupidly declared against Russia, France and Britain, at that time also allies and very powerful, and one in particular, Britain, having dominion over the seas and countless colonies.

That's how, in a thousand years' time – thinks Berecche – this truly atrocious war, which now fills the whole world with horror, will be reduced to a few lines in the great history of mankind; and there will be no hint of all the little stories of all these thousands and thousands of obscure beings who are now disappearing, swept away in it, each one of whom will nevertheless have held the world, the whole world in himself and, for at least one brief moment in his life, will have been eternal, his soul filled with this earth and this sky glittering with stars and his own little home far, far away, and his dear ones, his father, his mother, his wife, his sisters, in tears and, perhaps, unknowing still and intent upon their games, his little children, far, far away. How many wounded, not picked up, dying in the snow, in the mud, collect themselves waiting for death and look straight ahead with pitiful, vain eyes, and can no longer see the reason for the violence which, in an instant, has shattered their youth and loves in their prime, once and for all, as though they were nothing! No trace. No-one will know. Who even now knows all the little, countless stories, one for each soul, of the millions and millions of men facing each other to kill each other? Even now, there are just a few lines in the bulletins of the General Staff: *we've advanced, we've retreated; three or four thousand dead, wounded or missing.* And that's all.

What will remain tomorrow of the war diaries in the newspapers, where only a minute part of these little, countless stories is barely sketched out in a few brief words? Those cockerels, those cockerels which crowed at dawn in a Belgrade deserted and bombarded by the Austrian guns, at the beginning of the war ... Oh, my dear cockerels, that's it, if Berecche could come back to the world in a thousand years' time to teach the history of a thousand years before, when all memory of the events which now seem so dreadful to us has been wiped out and the whole of this appalling war will, for the men of the future, be contained in a few lines, that's it, Berecche would like to remember you, dear cockerels, and say that you crowed at dawn, in Belgrade, as though nothing was wrong, among the bombs which exploded on the abandoned, smoking houses.

No: this is not a great war; it'll be a great slaughter; but it isn't a great war because it isn't based on and sustained by any great ideals. This is a war about economic interests; the war of a brutish people, grown up too quickly and too busy and know-it-all, which went on the attack in order to impose its goods and, well-armed and with claws out, its precious knowledge, on everyone.

At this last consideration Berecche gets up; frowning, he walks for a little while longer around his study; then he goes out into the passage; he sees that the door of his son's bedroom is ajar; he stretches out one hand and very gently pulls it open. Faustino is in bed with the blankets pulled right up to his nose; but his eyes are wide open in the dark of the little bedroom, still angry and bright with indignation. When he sees his father coming in he closes them at once and pretends to be sleeping peacefully.

Berecche watches him, frowning; he shakes his head, seeing all around how untidy the little bedroom is; then, with his hands in his pockets, as he prepares to leave, he says softly, drawing out the words in a tone which seems to be mocking his son, but which in reality expresses his own change of heart:

"Long live ... yes! Long live Belgium ... long live France ..."

VI

MR LIVO TRUPPEL

Teutonia, the eldest in the family, whom her mother always called Tonia for as long as she had her at home, and which is, what's more, what she herself has always wanted to be called by her two younger sisters and her brother and then by her husband, left home three years ago on her marriage to Mr Livo Truppel, a very decent and kindly man with no inclination for politics, a native of German-speaking Switzerland, but now no longer Swiss and even less German.

It wasn't Mr Truppel who gave himself that surname, or chose it for himself; it came to him from his father, who died years ago in Zurich; and he doesn't like it very much.

Perhaps there in Zurich the name Truppel meant something; but outside one's native land, that is, outside one's circle of friends, family and acquaintances what is a surname? When you're a stranger, being called Truppel is no different from being called anything else. If it weren't for the need to have your papers in order ...

As for himself, Livo within himself knows that he is a peaceful soul, without a surname, without civil status or nationality; he's a person with both eyes open, here as elsewhere, to the deceptive nature of things, which are certainly not as they seem if one moment they can be seen in one way and the next in another, according to your state of mind and mood. He does everything possible never to change his way of seeing things, and he contents himself with little because he can enjoy that little in peace and wisely, like the innocent pleasures of nature which, if truth be known, is the same for everyone and knows no native land or frontiers.

Candid as he is, and tender-hearted, Mr Truppel especially likes days of light cloud, those you get after rain when there is a smell of wet earth and in the damp light the plants and insects have the illusion that spring has come again. At night, he looks at those clouds which spread over the stars and blot them out only for them to appear once more against fleeting, deep patches of blue. Like his father-in-law he looks at those stars; he dreams dreamlessly, and he sighs.

By day Mr Truppel considers that in life he is a decent fellow. A decent fellow, and that's the beginning and end of it. Not in Rome, that is in Italy, or anywhere else: no, in life. And that's the beginning and end of it. Or rather, more precisely, a good clock- and watch-maker, in life.

Firmly ensconced within the bounds of his counter which, covered in spotless oilcloth stands inside the window of his shop in via Condotti, he fixes his loupe into his right eye and, bending over the tweezers fixed to his bench, he tries out over and over again, with inexhaustible patience, the many little tools of his most patient trade, files, saws and callipers, on the part needing repair, in the silence laced with the assiduous, sharp, light ticking of his hundred clocks.

It doesn't even enter his head as, with infinite delicacy, he uses those tiny little tools on the fragile, complicated mechanism of the clocks that, in that very moment, elsewhere, throughout the greater part of Europe, millions of men like him are using very different tools – guns, canons, bayonets, hand grenades – for work which is very different from his own of mending clocks; and that the silence vibrating here all around him with the sharp notes of that continuous, scarcely audible, ticking is rent in other places by the hideous boom of shells and mortars.

His world, his life, are concentrated there, during the day, into the case of a clock; just as, at night, the life of his spirit, freed now from almost all earthly passions, is engrossed in the contemplation of the harmony of very different spheres: the celestial ones.

Although Mr Truppel seems stupid, you could swear from the way he smiles when he turns round, recalled from his contemplation of the heavens, that he doesn't consider the firmament to be a system of clockwork.

So he was just like someone coming down from the clouds the other evening when, as he went out into the street to lower his outside shutter, he found himself being attacked by a crowd of demonstrators which, arriving like a whirlwind, hurled itself at his clockmaker's shop and, in a twinkling, smashed his shop sign, his folding shutters, his window, everything.

After his first shock at the crash of the breaking glass Mr Livo Truppel was not so much afraid for himself as for his brother, his partner in the clockmaker's and very different in nature from him: touchy, gloomy and bestial.

Very round and very blond, Mr Livo flung himself forward, trying to ward them off with his little fat, white hands, with his eyes full of tears, those eyes which usually have the limpid, smiling clarity of sapphires, to shout at those demonstrators that he was Swiss, not German, Swiss not German, Swiss, Swiss and had been in Italy for more than twenty-five years, and was the son-in-law of an Italian, a teacher, Mr Berecche. Yes, but who was he shouting it at? At the neighbouring shopkeepers who know him well and all know what a gem of a man he is. The damage done, the demonstrators had already moved on some time before, quite convinced of having performed an act which, if not exactly heroic, was certainly very patriotic. The damage itself didn't really amount to much. The trouble, the real trouble, was with his brother, whom Mr Truppel thought was still inside the shop, but instead wasn't there any longer. *Terteuffel!*,[31] he'd run after those demonstrators, in a furious rage.

Now what had happened, which for the peaceful Mr Truppel amounted to a simple misunderstanding between himself and the population of Rome because of his German surname (a deplorable misunderstanding, indeed, but not one to make too much of), would certainly not have led to serious upsets in the family if his brother hadn't recognised Faustino, his young brother-in-law, among that crowd of demonstrators.

It's true that his brother hasn't ordered him to leave his wife and conjugal home to go back to living with him in a separate house. No, but he has demanded and made him promise and swear that at least he will never set foot in his father-in law's house again, and that if his father-in-law comes one evening to visit his daughter, if he can't find an excuse on the spot to leave the house he won't speak to him apart from saying hello, and after saying hello to him he'll spit on the ground: like this!

Spit on the ground?

Yes, spit on the ground; like this!

Mr Truppel, deeply distressed, looked at his brother's spittle on the floor, and very nearly took a handkerchief out of his pocket to go and wipe it up.

"No! no! you have to spit on the ground", his brother shouted at him "spit on the ground. Like this!'

And he spat again.

In the name of all that's holy! He is quite incapable of spitting, he never spits, even into his handkerchief, like the decent fellow he is! Yes, very well, agreed: Mr Truppel promised and swore in order to placate his brother, but you know what value certain promises and oaths have once the first moment has passed, even for those they are made to.

In the meantime Mr Livo Truppel, with the best of intentions, resolves to go in secret to his father-in-law's to implore him not to come to his house, at least for some time.

But the day he goes there, he finds his father-in-law's house in such turmoil, and for such an unexpected reason, that Mr Livo Truppel decides it is prudent to go back home without anyone seeing him.

VII

BERECCHE REASONS

He's gone, they've both gone, vanished six days ago, Faustino and the other boy, Gino Viesi – vanished.

The little flat in the out-of-the way house, the peace dreamt of for those final years in that secluded, almost rural spot, with the patrician villa in front – that screen of cypresses there, hateful to the women who see it as an ill omen of death – but still lovely to look at, those cypresses, knowing nothing of the melancholy function mankind has assigned to them and they turn gold in the sun, the beautiful sun which comes in through the four windows overlooking the garden and spreads through the rooms; and they're still lovely by moonlight, in the evening, while the little fountain gurgles nearby ... oh, yes, the fountain; but who listens to it any longer? And is the sun shining? Who sees it? Who cares about the moon? Now, as soon as they hear the gravel crunching in the garden under someone's feet, all that they see out there in front, right before their eyes, are those hateful, bristling, gloomy cypresses.

"No ... no ... It's the caretaker ..."

And from a long way away the tears, screams and shouts can be heard; from as far away as via Nomentana "and, for goodness' sake, in times like this it gives respectable people a fright! ... Is this any way to behave?" A typical irascible passer-by, with his newspaper whose pages are entirely given over to news of the war open in his hands, stops and stops other passers-by.

"Is there a fight? What's going on? Are they killing each other over nothing?"

Two or three of them give in to their curiosity and run into the barely marked-out side-road, and two or three more follow them, but are baffled; they turn round to look at those, less curious or more prudent, who have stayed on the main road; they look around (what a wonderful smell of hay! it's like being in the country!); they make up their minds and come running as well: outside the gate they look with alarm at the four windows from which those tears, screams and shouts are pouring forth. What's going on? No-one moves. They're shouting and yelling in there; but all around everything is peaceful, and the caretaker

52

of the house, oh, there he is, peacefully eating. So it's nothing, then! Some misfortune, a death, perhaps?

"Oh, nobody even knows, and they're screaming like that?"

"What d'you mean, they've vanished?"

"Gone to fight? Where? In France?"

"It's nice, that villa! Is it for rent? Six flats? The rent won't be all that high. Oh, really, as much as that? That's why they haven't been let ... It's lovely, yes, in the sun ... a beautiful garden ... too far out, though ... almost in the country ..."

But good God, screaming like that ... It's the mother, isn't it?

"The fiancée?"

"No, that's the mother ..."

The caretaker makes a sign as if to say: ... "She's gone off her head ..." – and goes back to his meal. There really are madmen in the world, by God, with the war hanging over all our heads, wanting to go before they have to, as though it were a party they can't wait to get to ...

"No, this is why it is, if they've gone to France ..."

"Come on, it can't be France! France, my dear sir ..."

"Is defending herself after being attacked! The real danger for us ..."

"Oh come off it, because either on one side or the other ..."

"We're neutral, we're neutral ..."

"Oh let's go and get something to eat" concludes a workman, a typical Roman, philosophically.

If only it were possible! For six days they haven't eaten and haven't slept in Berecche's house.

Two unleashed furies, that's what his wife and his daughter Carlotta have become. Especially his wife. Her hair all dishevelled, screaming and howling endlessly until she chokes, she runs through the house with her arms flailing, as though seeking an outlet for her desperate grief. Carlotta runs after her; after her run the three poor spinsters, the Monsignor's sisters, who have come from the house opposite: all three identically thin; all three with their hair done identically, and all dressed in grey with a little black shawl over their chests for the death of the Holy Father; behind her, one after the other, with their lips drawn tight, their eyes wide open and full of pity, straightening the little shawls over their chests with restless hands, all three with a thimble on one finger, because they came running at the screams while they were sewing, and they are quite unable to comfort that mother.

"Mrs Berecche ..." says one.

And another says:

"But Mrs Berecche ..."

And the third:

"But my dear Mrs Berecche ..."

The mother, in her despair, can't listen to anything: she screams and screams until she is hoarse, raising her arms and shaking her hands in a frenzy as soon as someone tries to say something to her. Oh! Lord bless us and keep us. Lord bless us and keep us! Even Monsignor, who came yesterday, met with the same reception.

The servant ... do the sweeping? She snatched the broom from her hands and ran after her to hit her over the head with it! She threw pillows, blankets, sheets into the air from the beds which the servant had started making; she snatched the table cloth from the table which had been laid for a meal: the plates, glassses and bottles crashed down onto the floor, smashed to pieces ... If she could at least see poor Margheritina's terror as she jumped up from her silent weeping in her usual little corner with her hands clenched and trembling in front of her chest! She sees nothing; she hears nothing; from time to time she hurls herself against the door of the study; she forces it open by battering it with her hands, her shoulders and her knees and she rages at her husband, rearing up at him with her fingers like claws in his face, as though she wanted to tear him to pieces, and she shouts at him, ferociously:

"I want my son! I want my son! Murderer! I want my son! I want my son!"

Berecche, who has aged twenty years in six days, says nothing: although he is deeply offended by her complete lack of restraint, he respects the torment in which that mother finds herself, which is the same as his own. However, he is angered by the sheer, unbridled rage with which it is turned against him and his torment, too, almost turns to rage, almost explodes with the same ferocity. But he controls himself and looks into his wife's eyes with such piercing agony that she first of all opens wide her own crazed eyes and then, bursting into wild, heartbreaking sobs she clutches at his chest, rubs her dishevelled head on his chest and whimpers:

"Give me my son! Give me my son!"

And then Berecche, first with a silent heaving of his chest and shoulders, and then with a deep, painful sobbing in his nose, bends over and he, too, weeps on the grey, tousled head of his old, unloved companion.

For the whole of the first day – six days earlier – their anxiety had grown hour by hour, together with a deep sense of misgiving and a veiled irritation, both of which also gradually increased, at their son's lateness in coming home; a lateness which was all the more inexcusable and inexplicable because there were no more demonstrations in Rome which might have led them to think he had been arrested, like the last time; – then, that evening, rushing anxiously hither and thither to look for him, in places he might have stayed so late, in the cafés, at some friend's house, in Gino Viesi's furnished room – and the surprise, here, on learning that he, Gino Viesi, had also gone out that morning at seven, and hadn't been seen since; then the night, that first night when their son wasn't at home, with the house seeming empty and fearful, just as his mind was empty and fearful; and the hours went by one by one, slowly, eternally, with his anxiety made worse by his dismay at seeing them pass like that, one by one, waiting in vain at the window, haunted by thoughts of the roads his son might have taken, along which he was still perhaps walking in the night, going further and further away from his home, wretched and ungrateful child! but going where? Heading for where? – and then the dawn and the silence of the whole house, dreadful, with the women finally falling asleep amidst their tears, over there on the chairs, with their heads on the table, beneath the light which was still burning – oh, that yellow light in the dawn, and those bodies there, which gradually of their own volition had mercifully settled down, arranging themselves so as not to suffer so much, so that they at least could find some rest, even if their sleep was too troubled for their souls to find any! – and then, in the morning and for the whole of the following day, rushing around again, three or four time to the police headquarters, first to report the disappearance of his son and the other boy, so that an order to arrest them could be issued at once and put into general circulation; then to see if there was any news; and there was never anything! – all those nos ... that no of the freckled, red-headed policeman, even though that morning he seemed to have taken the matter seriously on hearing that perhaps it was a case of two young men who were trying to get to France to enlist in the Garibaldi legion;[32] and now nothing, he was all intent on something else now as though he didn't even remember the order that had been given; – and the reproaches, the aggression becoming more violent by the hour of his wife and his daughter Carlotta, because they were sure that Faustino and the other boy had run away because of him, but of course, because of him, the one who had oppressed his son from childhood with German method, with German discipline, with German culture, to the extent of making him conceive an unconquerable, undying hatred for Germany, may God damn her to all eternity! and – just recently, in front of that other boy who was mourning two of his brothers who had been killed, hadn't he had the gall to shout that Austria was completely within her rights to send those two brothers to the slaughter? Yes, him! – that was why they had run away, to give him a fitting reply, to find a fitting revenge for the feelings he had hurt of one of them and oppressed, of the other, right from his childhood: well, isn't all this enough? There is still more to explain why Berecche has aged twenty years in six days.

But it isn't enough just to say that he's aged.

Berecche now maintains that he doesn't suffer at all any longer, really not at all. At the most, yes, he can admit, he does admit that he can entertain the idea of his grief in the abstract. In the abstract, perhaps, yes. But not of his own grief as such. Of the grief of a father, in general, to whom the same has happened as to him. In reality, however, he feels nothing. He weeps, yes ... perhaps, but like a play-actor, like an actor on the stage, merely for the idea of his grief, not so that he feels it. He imagines he feels it and he shows it. What is there to be afraid of if he talks like this? The most convincing proof is this: that he rea-sons, he rea-sons; he is perfectly well, more than perfectly well able to reason.

"I'm telling you, by God, that I'm reasoning!" he shouts at good sleepy old Fongi, who has come from the beer-house to visit him. "I'm reasoning."

As though good, sleepy old Fongi was saying anything different.

"And things would be much worse if I, at least, didn't reason in this house! Have you seen them, have you heard them, those two furies? It's my fault! Go on, you tell me, you tell me as well that it's my fault! I'd be pleased, you know? I'd rise even further above all these tears, all these screams, proud in the certainty that I alone am still capable of reasoning, here, right here!"

And he strikes himself hard on the forehead.

"Right here, so as to feel pity for my accusers! right here to sympathize both with those two poor, unfortunate women and with this wretched Italy of ours, a woman like them, which will never have what is called a SENSE OF DISCIPLINE! But don't you see, don't you see what is happening in this wretched Italy of ours because she has opted for a measure of such harsh discipline – that is, neutrality? Your children run away! Their mothers shriek and shout! Do you think I'm not reasoning?'

Good old Fongi, with his big, fleshy nose, keeps his head down and looks at him as though afraid from over the platinum frames of his pince-nez. As a retired doctor, perhaps he thinks to himself that there is no clearer sign of madness than reasoning, or believing you're reasoning, at certain times. In any case, if not quite afraid, good old Fongi does at least seem dumbfounded, and doesn't reply either yes or no, however much Berecche fixes his angry gaze on him, expecting a reply in the affirmative.

"No? You're saying no?"

"Me? Really, I ..."

"Do you perhaps think that when Italy first announced her neutrality I turned on the government?"

"No, I don't think ..."

"But you must think, you must think, by God! I need to think right now, and there you are sitting in front of me like a dormouse!"

Good old Fongi gives himself a little shake; he hastens to say to him: "Yes, go ahead, think ..., if it does you good ..."

"You have to think with me!" Berecche shouts at him. "You have to think that there and then I was prompted by a feeling of loyalty, do you understand? A feeling of loyalty towards that nation which had taught me DISCIPLINE, which ... – do you know what that means? – It means curbing, curbing, stifling, if need be, your natural feelings, as a father, as a son, all the natural feelings that deny constraints! Do you understand? Curbing nature which rises up against reason. Do you understand? But at once I saw the error of my ways; I understood that the real discipline for us must lie in stifling this feeling of loyalty as well; and I've stifled it! And I've even reached the point of recognising that Germany acted rashly, do you see? That Germany was wrong, that Germany's lost her head ... I've even, I've even come to this!'

Good old Fongi shrinks more and more into himself, and his nose seems to grow bigger and bigger. Berecche looks at that nose and, bit by bit, he feels an unjustifiable irritation with that nose growing in him. What kind of a nose is that! What an unbearable reality that nose is! He hurls such a weighty confession at it and nothing, simply nothing, happens: it stays there quite still; it shows no emotion. It's as tranquil as it is voluminous. It shows no emotion. A real Roman nose!

"I've even come to this!" shouts Berecche. "And to admitting as well, if you like, that Germany has turned against us by helping Austria, on a mere pretext, in an offensive war which, breaking the pacts of alliance, was inevitably going to make Austria our enemy. The alliance with Austria was a discipline for us! Germany has shattered that discipline because, on declaring war, she should have understood that we could no longer be the allies of Austria; and even more that we had inevitably to be against Austria! I'd even come to this! And even to thinking that if we, too, started to take action, and if my son, either because he was called up early or because he was driven on by a feeling which I would then have been unable to oppose, had gone to fight as a volunteer, I would have gone as well, me, too, just as you see me, a volunteer at fifty-three years of age and with my huge belly, I'd have gone as well! But now do you see what my son has done? He wanted to set himself against me! He meant to set himself against me! And why? Because like all the others he doesn't know what discipline means! And he's set his poor mother against me, and his sister; and this should really scare you now, Fongi, he's also set me against myself! Yes he has, because in me there's also a father who's weeping, and at whom I, who know what discipline means, am forced to shout: 'Come off it, you buffoon, don't cry, because you're wrong to cry!' Let the others cry! I'm not crying, I won't cry any longer, not even if the news comes, you understand? that he's dead! Not just that; but I tell you this, and I tell you loud and clear so that it can be heard as well by those two furies out there who would like to stop me from reasoning, coming here and shouting at me that they want their son or their fiancé from me, as if I were as mad as them; I tell you this: that now I'm on Germany's side again, yes I am, I'm telling you loud and clear, on Germany's side again, on the side of Germany which has probably committed an act of folly, indeed has done so for certain, but you see what a magnificent sight she still offers to the rest of the world? She's aroused the whole world against her and she's keeping it at bay! They're all powerless against her power! What a sight! And you want to demolish her? to destroy her? Who does? France, rotten to the core, Russia with her feet of clay, Britain? And are they worth more than her? What are they worth by comparison with her? Nothing! Nothing! No-one can defeat her!"

Oh at last! good old Fongi with his big nose wakes up all of a sudden from his torpor, which has been so battered, crushed and bludgeoned by the ferocity of the invective. In order to protest? No. He has news, news which he has been clutching to himself since he arrived and which, under the onslaught of all those tears and shouts, he has not yet found a way of delivering.

"I" he says "have here a letter from Faustino."

It's a miracle if Berecche doesn't drop down all of a heap in a dead faint. He turns very pale, and then all of a sudden purple in the face; he flings himself on Fongi as if Fongi were trying to get away:

"You?" he shouts at him. "A letter? from Faustino?"

And he weeps and laughs and shakes all over and runs stumblingly to shout in the passage:

"There's a letter ... a letter from Faustino! ... come quickly! ... Margheritina, Margheritina, bring Margheritina as well!"

And while his wife and Carlotta with Margheritina by the hand burst panting and trembling with impatience into the study, with his hands shaking he snatches the letter from Fongi's hands and tries to read it out.

"Sent to him."

"To you?"

"Yes ..."

"*Dear* ... here we are ... *Dear Mr* ... oh, God ... *Dear Mr Fongi* ..."

He can't go on. His eyes, his voice, his breath, even his legs fail him. He drops into a chair and hands the letter to Carlotta for her to read.

The letter is dated from Nice, and reads like this:

58

Dear Mr Fongi,

I know the great affection you have for my father and I'm writing to you to ask you to go and see him as soon as you receive this letter to tell him what he has probably guessed by now, with what anger and grief I leave you to imagine.

But please tell him, Mr Fongi, that I haven't come here to fight for France. He will be pleased at that! I've come here because I'm convinced (and I wish to God I was wrong!) that Italy, always the 'maidservant' and now without masters, will do nothing. The two she used to have – one of them hateful and who has always treated her badly and the other who always appeared to protect her, little old lady in decline as she is – have both, all of a sudden, without even dismissing her, without even telling her that they could do without her services, left her to her own devices and started to manage by themselves. Now poor Italy, who isn't even sure that she's been dismissed, doesn't know what to do or where to go. She's afraid of her old masters, and she's afraid of taking service with new ones which via the employment agencies, called Embassies, are asking for her and making her pressing offers. Which way should she turn, among those who tell her to stretch out this arm or that to take back from here and from there what used to be hers and everyone has taken from her? The poor lady in decline is quite incapable of being alone, by herself, used as she has now been for so long to serving masters for little reward in the apartments of her ancient, magnificent, airy house, full of sun, in a pleasant and flower-filled setting. There are many beautiful things, I know, and many great and glorious things in this ancient house, which the poor lady in decline has turned into a boarding-house; but there are also sad things and a deep sense of affliction, especially in the souls of this lady's sons, born as servants. Their mother has brought them up to be prudent, to be tolerant, to pretend not to understand or to hear; even to accept peaceably, if that is what happens, a slap by way of a tip, replying with a fine bow: – Thank you, sir! – ; she has brought them up to wear all liveries without blushing, as though each were the outfit which best became them, to brush away without embarassment from the folds of each of them the marks of the kicks they've received, and to take great care when drawing up the accounts, as often, alas, poor mother, they've come out wrong, to her detriment. Well then, Mr Fongi, tell my father that I'm here in France, not for France, with some of my companions – not many, oh, not many! – but just to demonstrate that in the midst of all that prudence and tolerance, and all that astuteness used to get the accounts right and that uncertainty about which livery it is best to wear at the moment, there is, even in Italy ... nothing really, a bit of wasted youth, and a bit of youth which doesn't know how to do the accounts or to be astute and prudent, in short, a bit of real youth. Our mother Italy doesn't need it, perhaps won't need it, and it may harm her internally; we've come here to fling it into action for her. My own little mother will say: – What do you mean? And I wasn't there, and aren't I a mother as well? And I need you! – That's true, mother, but just think that this is a time when all little mothers, like their sons, have to feel that they too are the little daughters of a greater mother. I'm here for you, if I've come here for this great mother we have in common, although perhaps at this moment you believe the opposite.

Kiss her hand for me, Mr Fongi, and assure her that I will send news often; comfort my father, who is perhaps suffering so much that he can't forgive me; kiss my sisters and tell Carlotta that Gino is here with me and will write her a long letter tonight. To you, Mr Fongi, I send my warmest thanks and my respectful and cordial greetings.

Your devoted FAUSTO BERECCHE

They're all in tears

They've been crying quietly during the reading so as not to miss a syllable. Now that the letter is finished, they continue to weep quietly for a little longer, as though not to disperse the echo of a distant voice.

Fongi murmurs, softly, almost to himself:

"So noble ... so noble ..."

In the end, Berecche jumps to his feet feeling suffocated, and crying out hoarsely flings himself on his wife; he clasps her in his arms, once more bends his face over her head, and both of them, clasped together like that, weep bitterly, trembling with sobs. Carlotta embraces Margheritina and they too weep bitterly. Good old Fongi, for his part, twists and turns to pull his handkerchief from the back pocket of his long frock-coat. In the end his big, tranquil nose has been deeply moved, and he blows it several times, loudly, repeating each time and nodding his head with deep conviction:

"So noble ... so very noble ..."

60

VIII

IN THE DARK

That evening when the caretaker of the house has turned out the light on the stairs and the garden is in darkness Berecche, wary and distraught and keeping his head well down re-opens the main door which the caretaker has just closed and calls him:

"Psst! Psst!"

The caretaker, who isn't expecting it, turns round almost scared; Berecche beckons him to come over in silence, without making too much noise on the gravel, and begins to talk to him in great secrecy:

"Well, for less than six hundred ..." says the caretaker at a certain point.

"Keep your voice down!"

"Because the Government has already requisitioned them from all the dealers ... at least so they say ... You know what it's like at times like this ..."

"Yes, of course; but for six hundred lire ..."

"Oh, a good pony, yes ... even a saddle-horse ..."

"But it has to be a saddle-horse!"

"You want it for ... ?"

"Keep your voice down!"

"A saddle-horse, certainly ... you'll find one for six hundred lire ..."

"On which, for the moment, I'll put down a deposit ... of two hundred ... or possibly two hundred and fifty lire ... like this ... Because I hope to be able to use it, but just in case I can't ... well, I'll only lose the deposit ... But please keep it a secret ... don't tell anyone. Deal with the matter yourself."

And Berecche, distraught, keeping his head well down and on tiptoe goes back into the house and leaves the caretaker there in the darkness of the garden, rooted to the spot with amazement at that mysterious commission to buy a horse given to him in such secrecy, in the dark, by the sole tenant of the house, a good and worthy man and a man of learning ... well! A saddle horse ... and no-one must know about it ...

After closing the main door very quietly and going back into his flat Berecche, still on tiptoe, crosses the corridor, shuts himself in his study, sits down at his little table, takes a piece of paper from his brief-case and begins to write:

To His Excellency the Minister of War – Rome: he raises the index finger of the hand holding the pen and places it on his lips. He meditates at length.

He has clearly in mind what he wants to ask of H. E. the Minister of War; but he is uncertain about the precise military terms. Does one say *Voluntary Mounted Guides Corps*, or something else? He'd better find out first from the War Ministry. And then, since he has to declare his age – fifty-three – wouldn't it be better to send a medical certificate saying that he is physically fit and healthy with his request? He can get it from Fongi tomorrow.

"No, not from Fongi ... not from Fongi ..." he murmurs. It must be kept secret from everyone. And then, he's given Fongi such very clear proof that he is in full possession of his reason and shouted at him with such vehemence that he is once more entirely on Germany's side ...

"No, not from Fongi ..."

Except that if he goes to see some other doctor who isn't his friend, can he be sure of getting this certificate that he is physically fit and healthy? There's his heart ... for some time now his heartbeat has been irregular; his heart is tired and sometimes his head is so heavy ... Who knows! He'll go first to see another doctor; if he can't get the certificate he'll appeal to Fongi, asking him to keep it a secret. Berecche, too, wants to go to war.

He puts the headed piece of paper back in his brief-case, gets up and goes over to one of his bookshelves; he takes down a Hoepli manual on *Horse-riding*;[33] goes back to sit at the little table; leans his elbows on it, takes his head between his hands and immerses himself in a preparatory reading:

CHAPTER ONE

Horse-riding: history and advice for beginners

The next day he's at the *Riding School* in via Po.

With one bundle under his arm (his leather riding boots and a riding whip, bought just now) – and another, smaller one in his hand – (his spurs) – Berecche presents himself before Mr Felder, the riding master.

"A crash course? But, may I ask, has Sir already had some experience of riding?"

Berecche shakes his head.

"No."

"Well, then?" Mr Felder exclaims with a smile of pity and wonder. For a short while he looks at that solid, square, sober figure of a man standing frowning in front of him; then, after asking permission, feels his leg muscles, which really are a bit flabby, really a bit thin in proportion to his ample trunk; he takes him by the hand – (*if I may*) – and invites him to bend his knees, keeping his feet together and balancing on the tips of his toes.

"I'll hold you."

Berecche, frowning more than ever, shakes his head again; he rejects the hand; he's done that exercise at home, locked away in his study; and now he performs it by himself, without help, once, twice, three times, with suppleness, with his eyes closed, in front of Mr Felder, who says approvingly:

"Ah, good ... good ... very good ..."

Berecche straightens up and informs Mr Felder, who is more and more astonished at the sombre way in which this new client speaks to him, that he has studied all night and therefore, as far as theory is concerned, he can say he's already firmly in the saddle. He points to the wooden exercise horse standing on a spot in the arena and makes the gesture of brushing it aside with his hand, to show that he can do without it because, in theory, he already knows all the positions and exercises and manoeuvres of the horse, set paces, half-pace, parade, pesade, pirouette ...

"A bit of practice, just a bit of quick practice" he concludes. "Look, I've brought this pair of riding boots with me. I'll put them on. Let me mount and let's try straight away, even on a horse that's a bit restive ... lively, I mean. It'll be better! It doesn't matter if I fall off."

Mr Felder tries to raise a number of objections; but Berecche interrupts him, repeating each time: "I'm telling you it doesn't matter if I fall off!" in such a peremptory tone that in the end he shrugs his shoulders and yields to the wishes of his strange client.

That first time Berecche doesn't fall off; but if wants to do it all his own way why on earth has he come to a riding stables? If he carries on like this he'll break his neck not once but ten times over, and once is enough. He doesn't care? But he, Mr Felder, cares as he doesn't want the responsibility; because in his school ...

"Look," he adds, "go gently, to begin with, in the English style."

"Which means?" asks Berecche from up on his horse, breathless and scarlet in the face.

"Well it means", Mr Felder resumes, "that as you know there is the Italian style of riding and the English style of riding. Try going gently, in the English style. Look, sit with a bit of your weight on the stirrups ... like this ... and make yourself rise and fall with the motion of the horse ... of course, leaning forward a bit with your head and body ... like this, go on, towards the neck of your mount ... not too much ... I'm saying that, you know, to stop your head from being shaken around too much ... I see that ... yes, you're a bit flushed ..."

"Oh, don't worry about that!" exclaims Berecche. "Well then let's go ahead and try in the English style ... Come on, let go of the bridle ..."

"Gently does it, to begin with ..."

"Let go, I tell you!"

The riding master lets go; the horse sets off at a gallop, and then Berecche ... oh, God ... oh, God! ...

"Keep firmly in the saddle! ... keep firmly in the saddle!" – Mr Felder shouts, running after him across the arena.

Berecche bounces around awkwardly, wobbles, sways to and fro and in the end falls off with a crash, with one foot still in its stirrup so that the horse drags him some way over the arena.

Nothing! He's done nothing to himself ... But the English style doesn't work!

"I'm telling you it's nothing! I'm very pleased ... Nothing ... I hurt my foot a bit ... but it's better already ... The English style doesn't work! Let me get back up. I'll do better in the Italian style, like before. And give me my whip!"

Mr Felder takes a step backwards, putting the whip behind him.

"Oh, no whips, my dear sir!"

"Give me my whip, I say!"

"I'd have to be mad!"

"But do you realise that I wouldn't have fallen off if I'd had my whip?"

Berecche laughs, panting, from the back of the horse. He's really pleased, yes, even with the fall. It was a wonderful moment, a great joy to him, to be galloping along and bouncing around like that: he thought of Faustino, of the war, of Faustino charging with his bayonet against the Germans and ... he wants to be off and away, at a gallop, with him, into the fray with his eyes closed. He wants to feel the same joy again now.

"Come on, stop fussing, give me the whip!"

He moves up on his horse; leans over; snatches the whip from behind Mr Felder's back; and he's off, whipping up his horse, off again at a gallop across the arena, with his eyes closed, plunging back into the violent vision of the Garibaldi legion at the charge, with Faustino at their head. And the faster his boy goes in front of him in his red shirt and with his bayonet fixed, the harder he whips his horse; onwards! onwards! long live Italy! Oh, how red those shirts are! A bit of youth ... A bit of wasted youth!

Who is shouting like that in the arena? ... Oh ... everything's whirling around! ... Who's running up? What on earth? Lying here? What happened? They're shouting, they're coming running ...

Berecche has crashed to the ground; flat on his face, with his forehead split open. He's gasping for breath, but he's full of joy; he doesn't feel any pain; he's just sorry for that good man Mr Felder, who's shouting with rage; he'd like to tell him that it's nothing; that he shouldn't worry about anything; that no-one will hold him responsible for the damage he's done to his head.

"Is it serious?" he asks the people who have come running to pick him up from the ground.

Seeing the way those people are looking at him, he understands that it is serious; but he is obviously unable to see his own face, with that open wound on his forehead; and he laughs, with his face covered in blood, to reassure those people.

"Well," he says "so we're off to the war?"

They take him by the shoulders and the feet and carry him outside; they lay him down in a cab to take him to the hospital.

"So off to the war, then?"

Contrary to every supposition that others might make, Berecche continues to reason; and he gives further proof of it, that evening, when, with a turban of bandages covering not just the whole of his head but also half his face, hiding both his eyes, they take him home from the hospital.

"I fell ... I fell ..."

That's all he says: not how or where he fell. He fell. But he reasons: so much so that he understands at once that if he says this without explaining how and where he fell his wife and his daughter Carlotta might suppose that he tried to kill himself. And so he adds:

"It's nothing ... I felt giddy in the street ... Don't be afraid ... my eyes are alright: it's just my forehead, a cut on the brows ... It's nothing. It'll get better."

He wants to be taken to his study and put to sit in his usual place for the evening. He only wants to have Margheritina with him. He sits her on one of his knees; he hugs her. He reasons; but it seems to him that Margheritina, if nothing else, will at least be able to see if the little red lamp in front of the little Madonna of the house opposite is alight; and he asks her if it is.

Margheritina doesn't reply. Berecche understands that his dear little Margheritina can't even see that; and he hugs her closer to his chest. Perhaps Margheritina doesn't even know that opposite there's a little house with a little Madonna at one corner and a little red lamp burning. What does the world mean to her? Well, now he can well understand. Darkness. This darkness. Everything outside can change; the world can become something other; a people disappear; a whole continent be redrawn; a war pass close by, to overthrow and destroy ... What does it matter? Darkness. This darkness. For Margheritina, always this darkness. And if Faustino is killed, tomorrow, there in France? Oh, then, for him as well, even without that bandage, with his eyes open again to see the world, everything will be darkness, always, like this, for him as well; but perhaps worse because he will still be condemned to see life, this atrocious life of men.

He again hugs his little blind daughter, forever enclosed in her dark silence, to his chest; he murmurs:

"And for this, my little girl, for all this let thanks be given to Germany!"

Rome, end of 1914, beginning of 1915

NOTES

1. 'Würstel' are German sausages; 'Krügel' are the stoneware beer-mugs decorated with figures.
2. Only in Germany, only in Germany/ There do I wish to die.
3. His surname (pronounced Bereke) is derived from the German verb 'berechnen', which means 'to calculate', 'to act in a calculating way'.
4. A wooden match.
5. On 2 August 1914 Italy declared her neutrality in the First World War, which had broken out on 28 July.
6. Austria began the hostilities by attacking Serbia, after the murder in Sarajevo of the Austrian Archduke Franz Ferdinand by the Bosnian teenager Gavrilo Princip on 28 June 1914. Germany declared war on Russia on 1 August, and on France on 3 August. Italy, then an ally of Austria and Germany, was not informed beforehand.
7. These were the Trentino and Venezia Giulia, lands between Italy and Austria which were then in Austrian hands.
8. Tunis was occupied by the French in 1881. Partly as a result of what Italy saw as an economic and military threat so close to the Sicilian coast, she joined the Triple Alliance with Austria-Hungary and Germany in 1882.
9. During Italy's war against Turkey for the conquest of Libya (1911–1912) it was claimed that France tried to help the Turks by smuggling arms to them.
10. In 1797 Napoleon ceded Venice to Austria by the Treaty of Campoformio, and in 1859 Napoleon III, who was then allied to the Kingdom of Sardinia, halted his attack on Austria–Hungary by an armistice agreed at Villafranca in 1859, so preventing the conquest of Venetia by the Franco–Piedmontese forces.
11. This is what Machiavelli (1469–1527) says in Chapter XXI of his treatise *The Prince*, about the dangers of neutrality.
12. Identified with via Antonio Bosio, where Pirandello lived in 1914 and to which he later returned before his death on 10 December 1936.
13. A large neo-classical villa in Rome, whose construction began in 1841.
14. Ghetina and Margheritina are both diminutives of Margherita.
15. This is the diminutive of Fausto, the name of Berecche's son. He is called 'Fausto' in the text when he breaks away from his father's control.
16. The reference is to the Franco–Prussian war of 1870, which ended with the defeat of France.
17. Berecche's love for this clock in the shape of a windmill links him to Cervantes' character Don Quixote.
18. References to the French Emperor Napoleon III (1808–1873) and the Piedmontese statesman Camillo Benso, Count of Cavour (1810–1861).

19. Patrice MacMahon (1808–1893) was the victor against the Austrians at the battle of Magenta (1859) in Italy's Second War of Independence, during which France was allied to Piedmont. During the Franco–Prussian War he was surrounded at Sedan (1870) and forced to surrender with his army to the Prussians. He was later President of the French Republic (1873–1879).

20. Here I have followed the text of the novella published in: L. Pirandello, *Novelle per un anno. Il viaggio. Candelora. Berecche e la guerra. Una giornata*, ed. L. Sedita, Milan, Garzanti,1994, p. 361, in which Russia is against Germany in Prussia and Poland, as this seems to be the correct version.

21. The famous German writer Johann Wolfgang von Goethe (1749–1832), author among many other works of *Faust*.

22. Barthold Georg Niebuhr (1776–1831), a Danish historian of German origin, and author of a 3-volume *History of Rome*.

23. Lucretia was the wife of Tarquinius Collatinus, and according to legend was raped by Sextus, son of Tarquinius Superbus. She took her own life after telling her husband about the rape. Again acording to legend Mucius Scaevola failed to kill the Etruscan king, Lars Porsena, and then showed his indifference to physical pain by holding his right hand in the fire.

24. The German poet and dramatist Johann Christoph Friedrich von Schiller (1759–1805); the German critic and dramatist Gotthold Ephraim Lessing (1729–1781); and the two great German philosophers Immanuel Kant (1724–1804) and Georg Wilhelm Friedrich Hegel (1770–1831).

25. The Adriatic regions, Istria and Dalmatia, had belonged to the Venetian Republic, and passed into Austrian control in 1797.

26. This city in Galicia, then in Austrian hands, was occupied by the Russians in August 1914.

27. Pope Pius X, born Giuseppe Sarto in the province of Treviso in 1835. He was elected Pope in 1903, and died on 20 August 1914.

28. Otto (912–973) was Duke of Saxony, King of Germany and from 962 Holy Roman Emperor with the title Otto I; Boleslas I (909–967), called Boleslas the Cruel, was Duke of Bohemia, and fought against Otto I but had to submit to his authority; Henry I (925–955) of Saxony became Duke of Bavaria; Louis the Child (893–911) was proclaimed King of Germany in 900.

29. Wilhelm II (1859–1941), Emperor of Germany and King of Prussia from 1888 to 1918; Franz Joseph (1830–1916), Austrian Emperor from 1848.

30. Victor Emanuel III (1869–1947) King of Italy from 1900 to 1946.

31. 'Devil take it'.

32. A legion of Italian volunteers led by Garibaldi's nephew (also Giuseppe).

33. A reference to the Milanese publishing house specializing in technical and scientific publications founded by the Swiss publisher Ulrico Hoepli (1847–1935).